The glass shattered in Bannion's tightening fist. He stood and stepped into the aisle between the two rows of booths. "Hello, punk," he said to Jones.

Jones turned quickly, his lips drawing tight against his teeth. He looked up at Bannion and some of the bored sullen toughness left his face. "This isn't any business of yours, Bannion," he said.

Bannion took the lapels of Jones' coat in one hand and pulled the man close to him. "You tell me what my business is, punk," he said in a low, trembling voice. "You tell me all about it."

Jones wet his lips and tried to meet Bannion's eyes. "I-I got nothing to tell you Bannion," he said.

Bannion held the slack of Jones' coat in one big hand. He raised his arm slowly and lifted the man up to his toes...

THE BIG HEAT

William P. McGivern

BERKLEY BOOKS, NEW YORK

THE BIG HEAT

A Berkley Book / published by arrangement with
Dodd, Mead & Company

PRINTING HISTORY
Dodd, Mead edition published 1953
Berkley edition / August 1987

ISBN: 0-425-10112-6

A BERKLEY BOOK ® TM 757,375
Berkley Books are published by The Berkley Publishing Group,
200 Madison Avenue, New York, New York 10016.
The name "BERKLEY" and the "B" logo
are trademarks belonging to The Berkley Publishing Corporation.

PRINTED IN THE UNITED STATES OF AMERICA

10 9 8 7 6 5 4 3 2 1

One

IT WAS EIGHT o'clock at night when the phone rang. A detective lifted the receiver and said, "Homicide, Neely speaking." He listened a moment, frowning slightly through the smoke that curled up from the cigarette in his lips. "All right, we'll send someone out right away," he said. He put his cigarette on the edge of the scarred desk and picked up a pencil. "What's your name and address?" he said. He put the cigarette back in his mouth and began writing on a pad at his elbow.

There were three other detectives in the large, shabby, brightly lighted room. Two of them were playing cards at a desk beside the long bank of green filing cases. The third, a tall, well-groomed man with a long intelligent face, paced the floor with his hands clasped behind his back. On a bench just inside the wooden counter that ran the length of the room sat a uniformed patrolman and a Negro. The Negro, who was young and solidly built, seemed to be trying to shrink inside his cheap, brown suit.

The card players stopped their game and glanced at Neely, who was frowning at the information he was taking down. One of them, a man named Carmody, with tired, sagging features and thinning hair, glanced at the windows. Rain was rolling down them in slow, level waves. "You might know a job would come along," he said. His partner, Katz, a big man with the roughed-up features of a preliminary fighter,

1

shrugged. "They always do on nights like this," he said in a mild voice.

The pacing detective grinned at them. "Unfortunately, I've got this matter to handle," he said, jerking his head at the solidly-built Negro. "Otherwise I'd be glad to accompany you gentlemen on a little trip in the rain."

"Yeah, Burke, I'll bet you would," Carmody said.

The detective on the desk, Neely, a small, red-haired man with a terrier's face, put the phone down and swung about in the swivel chair. He glanced at the clock hanging above the filing cabinet. "When did Bannion say he'd be back?" he said.

They all looked up at the clock. "About eight," Burke said. It was then a moment after. "He was at the Nineteenth when he called to say he was coming in."

Neely drummed his fingers on the desk, frowning.

"Well, what's up?" Burke said.

"That was Tom Deery's wife," Neely said. "He just committed suicide, she says. Shot himself."

"For God's sake," Carmody said.

"He was in the Superintendent's office, wasn't he?" Burke asked rhetorically.

"What would he want to do a thing like that for?" Katz said, in his mild voice.

"Maybe he was tired of paying bills," Carmody said.

"Hell, that's no reason."

"Okay, I don't know," Carmody said, rubbing his tired face. "He didn't tell me his plans."

Neely glanced at the clock. "I'm going to wait a few minutes for Bannion," he said. "They'll want a full report on this one."

"Yeah, they always do when it's a cop," Burke said, resuming his pacing. Carmody lit a cigarette and dropped the match on the floor. The silence was disturbed only by the rain drumming against the windows. It was a troubled, uneasy silence.

A cop's death is one thing: it means black bunting looped over the door of his station house for a week or so, a few paragraphs in the papers, and a note to the family from the Mayor and his Captain. A cop's suicide is another matter. It can mean that the man was a weakling, a neurotic, a fool—in any case no one to have been safeguarding the lives and properties of other citizens. Or it can mean something even less wholesome, something potentially dangerous to the entire, close-knit fabric of the department.

"He was a nice guy," Burke said, pacing slowly. "A nice, straight guy."

"That's what I always heard," Carmody said. He looked up at the clock. "How come his wife called us, Neely?"

"She knows the police business," Neely said. "She called Central first and then us. She knows we take a look at most suicides. Central should be giving the call to the district any second now."

They were all silent again, glancing up at the police speaker on the wall. It had been quiet for a few minutes. Now, as if Neely's comment were a cue, it coughed metallically, and the police announcer's flat voice said, "Nine Eighty, Nine Eighty One, report."

"That's his district, I think," Carmody said. "Deery lived in West, in the Ninety Eighth, didn't he?"

"Yeah, that's right," Katz said. "On Sycamore Street. They're sending the wagon and the street sergeant's car out there."

The police announcer connected with the cars he had asked to report, gave his orders: "Hospital case, Fifty Eight Sixty One Sycamore Street."

"Hospital case," Neely said with a short laugh. He drummed his fingers on his desk and looked up at the clock.

The double doors of the Homicide Bureau swung open and a young man in a damp trenchcoat came in and walked around the counter. He glanced at the three detectives, noticing their expressions. "What's up?" he said.

"Tom Deery's wife just called," Neely said. "She says Tom killed himself about fifteen or twenty minutes ago. Shot himself."

Burke said, "You knew him, didn't you, Bannion?"

"Sure, I knew him," Dave Bannion said slowly, as he took off his trenchcoat and dropped it over the back of a chair. He was a large, wide-shouldered man in his middle thirties, with tanned, even features and steady gray eyes. Standing alone he didn't seem particularly big; it was only when Burke, a tall man himself, strolled over beside him, that Bannion's size became apparent. He stood inches taller than Burke, and his two hundred and thirty pounds were evenly distributed on a huge, rangy frame.

"Did Deery have any kids?" Burke said.

"No, I don't think so," Bannion said. He had known Deery in the perfunctory way he knew dozens of men in the police department. Deery had been a slender, graying man, with an intelligent, alert, but unrevealing face. Bannion had passed him in the hall, had said hello to him, had checked clerical matters with him on several occasions, and that was the extent of their relationship.

He glanced at Neely. "I'll take a ride out there," he said. "Burke might as well come along, too."

Burke nodded at the Negro. "I'm working on this job, Dave. Want me to drop it?"

"What is it?"

"Well, he might be the character who killed that gas station attendant in the North East last week. The Tenth detectives picked him up and sent him down."

"I didn't kill nobody," the Negro said, standing, his large, bony hands working spasmodically. His head turned, his eyes touched each face in the room, frightened, helpless, defiant.

"Sit down," the uniformed cop said to him.

Burke smiled pleasantly at Bannion. "I could find out in ten little minutes if you'd just let—" He stopped at the look on Bannion's face. "Okay, okay, it was just a stray thought," he said, shrugging elaborately.

"There won't be any of that stuff on my shift," Bannion said.

"Okay, *okay,*" Burke said.

Bannion walked over to the Negro, who seemed to sense that he had got a break of some kind. "We just want the truth from you," Bannion said. "If you've done nothing wrong you've got nothing to worry about. But if you have we'll find it out. Remember that."

"I done nothing wrong," the Negro said excitedly. "I was walking——"

"All right, I'll talk to you when I get back," Bannion said. "I don't have the time now. Burke, you stick at it." He glanced at Katz and Carmody. "All right, any volunteers?"

Carmody sighed. "Let's go," he said. "Katz's wife would raise hell if he got his feet wet tonight."

"Ha, ha," Katz said expressionlessly, and began dealing himself a hand of solitaire.

The Homicide Bureau was on the first floor of City Hall, flanked by the rackets detail and the vice squad. Bannion walked down the long wide dusty hallway, a step ahead of Carmody, nodding occasionally to detectives and patrolmen coming in for duty. He left the building by a side door and went through the Hall's cold and drafty concourse to the parking area reserved for police cars. As they were crossing the sidewalk, the rain hit both men in a driving shower and they grabbed their hatbrims and ran for it. Bannion slid in behind the wheel of his car and opened the right hand door for Carmody, who climbed in panting and shivering.

"You always get 'em on nights like this, eh Dave?" he said disgustedly.

Thomas Francis Deery had lived in a West side, three-flat apartment building, on a tree-bordered, residential street. When Bannion got there a red car and wagon from the Ninety Eighth were parked in front of the building, and a uniformed cop was standing in the vestibule. It was raining hard, but half a dozen persons were huddled together on the sidewalk watching the police cars and the building.

Bannion nodded to the man in the vestibule, who wore a wet, shining, rubber slicker over his uniform. "It's on the first floor, sarge," he said, tossing Bannion a salute.

"Thanks," Bannion said. The door of Deery's apartment was open, and two big men from the wagon were standing just inside the hallway, chatting together while rainwater dripped from their slickers onto the highly-polished wooden floor. A tall man in a black overcoat came out of a door to the right of the hallway, and said to them, "Okay, you can have him now."

"Hold it a minute," Bannion said. He didn't know the man in the black overcoat, but assumed he was a detective from the Ninety Eighth. "We're from Homicide."

"You had a ride for nothing," the man in the black overcoat said, smiling. "It's nothing for you boys. I'm Karret,

Ninety Eighth Detectives.'' Bannion introduced himself and
they shook hands. "I heard about you," Karret said, still smiling. He looked Bannion up and down and from side to side.
"I heard you were big, and I heard right."

Bannion was used to this sort of thing, and it didn't bother
him. He'd always been the out-sized one, in high school and
college, even on football teams. He smiled at Karret, and then
said, "What's the deal here?''

"He's in here," Karret said, and led the way into the room
on the right of the hallway.

The dead man lay on his side, curled up in front of a desk
that was placed under a curtained window. Bannion knelt and
inspected the wound in his right temple, and the gun in his
right hand. The wound was ugly, and the revolver was a
nickel-plated thirty-two with black handgrips. After a moment
or so, Bannion stood and glanced around the room, automatically noting its contents and arrangement. There was the
desk, turned sideways to the window for better light, with a
portable typewriter on it, and a wooden correspondence box
half-full of papers. A large, comfortable reading chair was in
one corner, a floor lamp beside it, and a row of bookcases
stood against the opposite wall. Three Audubon prints were
hung above the bookcases, and a large, glass ashtray with half
a dozen cigarette stubs in it was on the desk beside the typewriter. It was a pleasant room, a luxury that a man without
children could provide for himself in a small, city apartment.

"It looks like he was kneeling down when he shot himself,''
Karret said, nodding at the body. "The way he's curled up, I
mean.''

Bannion checked the window, found it locked. He turned
away from it and glanced about the room. "Where's Mrs.
Deery?'' he said.

"She's in the living room."

"What did she have to say?''

"Well, she says he came in here after dinner. She stayed in
the kitchen cleaning up, and then went into the living room to
listen to the radio. About half an hour later she heard a shot.
She came in and found him just like he is now.''

"Was there any note?''

"No, not a thing.''

Bannion pushed his hat back on his forehead and sat down at Deery's desk. He glanced through the papers in the correspondence box. They were bills chiefly, a few sales letters, and one personal note from a friend in Hashville, dated a week previously. The friend, whose name was Mort Chamberlain, apologized for not answering Deery's letter of four months back; he'd been busy with the office and his family, he explained, and then made a joke about his laziness probably being the real reason. There wasn't much more in the letter. It seemed to be one of those cheerfully futile attempts to keep something going that had stopped a long, long time ago.

"I told you you had a ride for nothing," Karret said.

"Yes, this isn't anything for us," Bannion said. "Mrs. Deery have any guesses about why he did it?"

"She said he hadn't been feeling well lately and was worried about it," Karret said.

"Well, I guess that's the answer," Bannion said. He went through the drawers of the desk carefully, not looking for anything in particular, simply following his usual methodical working habits. He found two insurance policies, each in the amount of five thousand dollars, and made out to Mary Ellen Deery, the stubs of two checkbooks, with all entries written in a neat small hand, and an envelope containing a few departmental circulars clarifying policies in regard to police pensions, time off, and so forth. There was also a box of paper clips, several pencils, and a box of stationery. That was all. Bannion closed the drawers, after replacing everything as he had found it, and walked over and glanced at the volumes in the book cases. Most of them were in standard sets, history, biography, the novels of Scott and Dickens, and a selection of book club premiums.

There was a shelf of travel books he noticed, all of them well-worn. He picked out a couple of them, and flipped through the pages, wondering idly at this bent of Deery's. There were penciled notes in Deery's handwriting in the margins, and Bannion immediately became more interested. There was nothing more potentially revealing, he felt, than a man's honest, impulsive reactions to a book. However, Deery's comments were fairly routine. Of a description of bullfighting, he had observed, "Not for me!!" and of vulgar statues at Pompeii, he had written, "Just like a Peep Show."

"He read a lot," Karret said, nodding.

"Apparently." The books struck Bannion as curious. He glanced through a few more of them, turning them to the light to read Deery's marginal comments, before returning them to their shelf. They weren't the books one might expect to find in a police clerk's library. In fact, a library of any kind in a police clerk's home was rather unusual.

"Are you going to talk to his wife?" Karret said.

"I think I'd better," Bannion said. "How's she taking it?"

"She's fine, no trouble at all. A real sensible woman." He nodded toward a closed door on the opposite side of the hallway. "She's in there, in the living room, quiet as you please."

"I'll go in and see her," Bannion said, and walked out of Deery's study. He tapped on the living room door and a light, controlled voice said, "Come in, please."

Bannion turned the knob and entered a very clean, very neat room, furnished with fragile elegance, and lighted softly by two floor lamps. Mrs. Deery was seated on a brocaded sofa, her hands folded quietly in her lap. The legs and back of the sofa were bright with gilt, and the brocaded upholstery was a gleaming canary yellow; it made a cheerful, gracious frame for the woman. She turned her small head to him, and smiled slightly.

"Please come in," she said. "You mustn't apologize. I know this is necessary."

"Thank you," Bannion said. He sat down in an armless chair that made him uncomfortably aware of his size, and faced her across the low, mirrored coffee table. "I won't stay more than a few minutes, I promise you. My name is Bannion, Dave Bannion, and I knew your husband downtown."

Mrs. Deery listened attentively, her small head tilted to one side. She gave the impression of not wanting to miss one word he said. "I know Tom had many friends," she said quietly.

"Would you mind telling me what happened tonight, please?"

"No, of course not. I'm a policeman's wife, Mr. Bannion. I know this is necessary. Well, Tom came home at a quarter of six as usual. If you knew him you'll remember how punctual he always was. We had dinner, just the two of us, and then he went into his study. That's our extra bedroom. I did the dishes, and then came in here to sew and listen to the radio.''

While her voice, low and pleasing, fell into the silent, softly lighted room, Bannion tried to sort out his impressions of her, and of this clean, orderly little world in which Thomas Francis Deery had lived and died. He would like her as a witness on his side, Bannion thought. She was intelligent and controlled—if those words didn't mean about the same thing. Anyway she was clever enough to control herself, strong enough, too, and cleverness and strength are a reasonable facsimile of intelligence. Physically, she was small, slim, and well-cared for, with ash-blone hair, streaked with silver at the temples, and clear, fresh skin and eyes. She wore a black suit with a rhinestone clip on the right lapel, and a thin diamond wedding ring. Everything about her was meticulously arranged and ordered; her small black patent leather pumps shone glossily, her sheer nylons lacked even the suggestion of a wrinkle, and her nail polish and makeup looked as if it had been applied, and with great care, within the last fifteen or twenty minutes. and possibly it had, Bannion thought, with an odd quirk of annoyance.

"I heard the shot, of course, and for a moment, really only a few seconds, I suppose, I sat here, too surprised to move.'' Mrs. Deery moistened her lips and looked down at the backs of her slim white hands. "I called to Tom then but got no answer. When I went into the study I found him on the floor. He was dead. I called the police right away,'' Mrs. Deery said, looking up into Bannion's eyes.

"It must have been a terrible shock. Had your husband seemed worried or upset lately?''

"No, I wouldn't say that. I explained to the other detective about his health,'' she said. "That's the only thing I can think of. We have no other problems. There was enough money and we got along very well. Tom didn't make a great deal but his income was steady, even during the depression when we were just getting started, and we were able to save a little money. It must have been his health that worried him, Mr. Bannion. Three or four times in the last few months he complained of pains along his left side. He said it was probably indigestion when I suggested he see the police surgeon."

"Then he didn't go to a doctor?"

"Not that I know of, Mr. Bannion."

"Did he usually read every night?"

"Not every night, but he did enjoy reading a great deal."

"He was interested in travel books, I noticed."

Mrs. Deery smiled, a little girl's smile. "I really don't know, Mr. Bannion. I was never much for reading myself. You see, Tom was the brains of the family."

Bannion took out his cigarettes, but seeing no ashtrays about put them back in his pocket. Mrs. Deery noticed the gesture but said nothing. There was an ashtray in the study, and Tom Deery had apparently done his smoking there, Bannion decided. "Thanks for being so helpful," he said, standing. "If there's anything you need, anything at all, please get in touch with us, Mrs. Deery."

"Thank you Mr. Bannion. I appreciate your offer. It . . . it makes me feel less alone."

Bannion said goodbye to her and left her behind in the clean, graciously furnished room, still sitting on the brocaded sofa, hands folded quietly in her lap. He closed the door of the room and caught Carmody''s eye. "Okay, let's go," he said. They said goodbye to Karret, and went down the stairs and out to Bannion's car.

The rain was still falling. Bannion lit a cigarette and then stepped on the starter.

"Well, it's nothing for us," Carmody said, settling down comfortably.

"Yes, he shot himself, all right," Bannion said . . .

Downtown he typed out a detailed but informal report on Deery's death, and put it in an envelope for the Superintendent. The official report would come from Karret, since it was a district job with no homicide angle. A reporter from the *Express*, Jerry Furnham, came in and sat on the corner of his desk. Furnham was a veteran of the Hall, a bulky man in his early forties, with thinning black hair and a tough but amiable face. In his work he played ball most of the time, but no one pushed him around. "What's the story on Deery, Dave?" he said, taking out his cigarettes. "All Kosher?"

Bannion nodded, and took one of Furnham's cigarettes.

"He's been worried about his health, his wife said."

"Too bad. What was it? Heart? Cancer?"

"Heart, probably." Bannion tapped the envelope marked for the Superintendent. "There's my report on it, if you want to look it over."

Furnham shook his head. "Our district man in West got the details from Karret. It's not my story, of course. But the office wanted me to check it. Our man there is a live one from an Alabama school of journalism. The desk just wanted to be sure he hadn't missed anything—such as Deery's name and address."

Bannion smiled, wondering slightly at Furnham's interest. "Tell them not to worry," he said.

"Sure. Was there a note, by the way?"

"No, not a thing."

Furnham borrowed Bannion's phone to call his desk. After that he sauntered out. Bannion got through some paper work that had accumulated, and then went along to the cell block to talk to Burke's Negro. The man was frightened, but his story sounded reasonable to Bannion. Burke's case was a long way from airtight. He told Burke they needed more on it and went back to the office.

Neely and Katz were arguing about the coming elections. Carmody was asleep with his hands folded over his small paunch.

It was almost twelve; time to quit.

When his relief, Sergeant Heineman, lumbered in, Bannion told him everything was quiet, and got into his coat and went out to his car.

It had been a run-of-the-mill night, like a thousand he had known in the past. He felt comfortably tired as he followed the curving, shining Schuylkill out to Germantown, listening with only mild interest to a news program on the radio. It was good to be on his way home, he thought. Home to dinner, to Katie.

Two

BANNION SAT IN the kitchen with a scotch and soda before him and watched his wife, Kate, as she made dinner. He smiled as she put a steak into a very hot, lightly greased frying pan.

"How you squeeze steaks out of my salary is a source of wonder to me," he said. "At work they don't believe it. They insist you've got a private income, or something."

She sat down opposite him and took a small sip from his drink. "Well, enjoy this one then because it's the last of the month. And next year, when Brigid starts to school, you can kiss them goodbye until she gets out of college. Unless you become Superintendent in the meantime."

"Oh, that's inevitable. How was bedtime by the way?"

"The usual tug of war," Kate said, going to the stove to turn the steak. She was a tall, red-haired girl, with good-humored but very direct blue eyes, and very fair, flawless skin. She wasn't beautiful, although people thought she was at first because of her hair and complexion; but her features were very appealing in their liveliness, humor, and interest. Now, as she salted the steak, she was grinning slightly. "She had to go to the bathroom a few times, hear a couple of extra stories, and have a glass of water, before she finally went to sleep. She's angelic all day, but at night she's a holy terror."

Bannion raised his eyebrows. "That's the way I usually describe you," he said.

"Seriously, the book says to be patient but firm. You've tried that, I suppose?"

"The book, the book," Kate said. "It's very scientific and calm, but it doesn't work. Not with me anyway. The baby books never heard about Brigid, that's the trouble."

"The thing is, she's madly in love with me," Bannion said. "The Oedipus business, you know. Naturally she's jealous of you, as any sensible woman would be, and that's why there's conflict. Reasonable?"

"Yes, but I don't believe it," Kate said.

"Well, it's a little too pat, I guess," Bannion said. "It's like circumstantial evidence. If everything fits too well, look out. Come on, that steak's done."

"Here you are."

After dinner Bannion settled down in the living room to look through the papers. He was in an odd mood, one of curious, non-specific gratitude. It wasn't just a highball, the steak, the sense of pleasant relaxation. He glanced around the warm, slightly cluttered room. One of Brigid's dolls was on the radio, and a pull-toy and some books of hers were on the floor. Kate was sitting on the sofa, the sofa that needed covering he remembered, her feet curled under her, the lamplight touching her hair, her plain gold wedding band, her slim, silken legs.

He went back to his paper, his mood unresolved and unexplained. There was a story on Tom Deery on page three, a short story with a picture of the dead man. He read through it, remembering Deery as he had lain on the floor in his neat, orderly home, and his wife, who had seemed so fastidiously untouched by the messiness of his death. Bannion put down his paper and lit a cigarette. Deery's travel books, tracked with marginal notes, was an odd thing. Why the devil did people read travel books? To learn something, to kill time, to escape into a world of arm-chair adventuring. All of those reasons perhaps. Possibly Deery was simply bored, and used the books as a crutch to help him through the long evenings. Bannion smiled slightly and glanced at the bookcase beside his chair. There were his crutches then, comfortable, well-worn ones, with pages as familiar to him as the lines of his hands. They were travel books of a sort; they were volumes of philosophy,

and the world of ideas could be travelled and explored as well
as foreign countries, and strange jungles. Deery read about the
bull-fighting in Spain, while he read the spiritual explosions of
St. John Of The Cross, who was a Spaniard but no bull-
fighter. What was the difference? Why did one man read one
thing, the next man another? Well, there didn't have to be a
difference of course. Bannion read philosophy because it was
a relief from the dry and matter-of-fact routine of his own
work. I'm not trying to escape from anything, he thought.
Still you couldn't be sure; the need for escape might be un-
conscious. But he didn't think it was that. He was frowning
now, asking himself some of the questions he would have liked
to ask Deery. I read philosophy, he thought, because I'm too
weak to stand up against the misery and meaningless heartbreak I run into every day on the job. I'm no scholar. I
wouldn't touch Nietzsche or Schopenhauer with a ten-foot
pole. That's a frank, cheerful prejudice, nothing more. I don't
want to listen to idols being smashed, I want to read something which puts sense into life.

"Are you going to read tonight?" Kate said, noticing that
he was frowning at his books.

"No, I don't think so. Maybe for half an hour at most."

"Which one is it going to be?" she asked. "Croce or—
what's the German's name?"

"Kant, I guess," Bannion said. Deery, he thought, might
have been better off with these books than with descriptions of
the fertility charms in Pompeii. These were the men he, himself, had gone to for peace of mind. St. John Of The Cross,
Kant, Spinoza, Santayana. The gentle philosophers, the ones
who thought it was natural for man to be good, and that evil
was the aberrant course, abnormal, accidental, out of line
with man's true needs and nature.

"That's the one, Kant," Kate said. "Isn't it nice how I ram-
ble on whether you're listening or not? It must be a cozy little
background noise for your own thoughts."

"What? Oh, sure." He glanced at her, smiling. "You're
getting good. You're getting the names down fine. Kant,
Croce, whither will it end?"

Kate made a face at him, and said, "I look at their names

when I do the dusting, Smarty Pants. Don't be stuck-up."

"Go on, you're reading them the minute my back is turned," Bannion said, picking up his paper. Deery's wife, he thought, knew nothing of her husband's interests. She hadn't known he read travel books. That didn't indicate a very warm or sympathetic relationship. When a man takes to travel books it is something that a wife, if only in the light of self-interest, should consider thoughtfully, he thought.

Kate put her magazine aside. "Dave, didn't you get enough philosophy in school?"

"At the time it seemed like too much," he said. "I was interested in football then, and speculative discussion left me pretty cold. Probably——"

The phone rang, cutting off his sentence.

"Who could that be?" Kate said.

"I'll get it."

"Hurry. It's going to wake Brigid."

Bannion tip-toed past Brigid's closed door and shut the dining room door before picking up the phone. "Hello," he said.

"Mr. Bannion? Is this Mr. Bannion, the detective?" It was a woman's voice, low, faintly anxious.

"Yes, what is it?"

"Maybe I shouldn't have bothered you so late," the woman said. "I hope I'm not disturbing you."

"What is it?" Bannion said.

"My name is Lucy, Lucy Carroway. I was a friend of Tom Deery's. That's why I called you, Mr. Bannion." There was the sound of a faint, noisy conversation behind her anxious voice. "I just read that he killed himself, and I saw your name in the story. I looked you up in the telephone book, and that's how I got your number. I know it's late, Mr. Bannion, but I felt that I just had to talk to you."

"About what?"

"Well, about Tom," the woman said. "I've got to see you about him, about him killing himself."

"Won't it keep till tomorrow?"

There was a pause. "I suppose so," the woman said.

Bannion damned his conscience. He didn't want to go out, but he would, of course. "Okay, where can I talk to you?" he said.

"I'm at the Triangle Bar now. I work here. That's at Twentieth and Arch."

"I know the place." He glanced at his watch. It was one-twenty. "I'll be there before two, Lucy."

"Thanks, thanks a lot, Mr. Bannion."

He replaced the phone in its cradle and returned to the living room. Kate looked up at him inquiringly. Bannion shrugged. "Mysterious female wants to talk to me about a job I had tonight," he said. "Probably she's got it mixed up with a couple of other people she knew in Detroit or Oshkosh, but I've got to see her." He smiled and touched her cheek with the back of his hand. "Hell of a life, isn't it?"

"Oh, I'm used to it," Kate said, standing and smoothing down her skirt. "I'm getting to like it, as a matter of fact. The suspense is pretty heady. Will he come home for dinner? Will he be called out? Where's my wandering boy tonight?" She put her arms around him and hugged him tightly. "I'm okay, Dave, don't worry. I've got it good, I think."

"I'll hold that over your head someday," he said.

"How late will you be?" That was as much as she ever asked him about his work.

"Not long, baby."

"I'll wait up for you."

"Aren't you tired?"

"Sure, I'm tired." She looked up at him and smiled. "What's that got to do with it?"

"Okay, I'll see you in an hour or so then," he said. "And don't think I'm not flattered."

"You should be," she said.

He kissed her goodbye and went out to his car. He was still smiling slightly as he started back toward center-city . . .

The Triangle Bar was a small-time nightclub, choicely located between a burlesque house and a State Liquor Store. It was on Arch Street, a dreary skid row that stretched for about twenty blocks between the Schuylkill and Delaware Rivers. Here there were shooting galleries, Army and Navy stores and dozens of warehouses, clip joints, and small, weary shops. It was a depressing street, patently, determinedly small-time, with a quality of winking, guilty, rib-nudging lust about it.

Bannion parked under the glare of the Triangle's neon sign

and went inside. The long, oval bar, which imprisoned a colored trio on a tiny bandstand, was crowded with sailors, soldiers, and sharply dressed young men, who were covertly eyeing the chorines from the next-door burlesque house, hard, hennaed, heavily made-up girls who slipped in for a drink and a sandwich between shows. They wore wrappers over their shorts and bras, and sat together, talking shop and sipping their drinks. The young men wouldn't score with them, Bannion knew. The girls were a tough and practical lot, dead-tired most of the time from their four shows a day, and they wanted no part of sailors, soldiers, and nervous young men. They sipped their drinks, minding their own business, but their lures, the mascaraed eyes, the shaved, chalk-white legs, the ladies-of-midnight aura, all smacking of the illicit, kept the young men hanging around, kept them in a state of noisy, nervous excitement. The girls might go for a calm, sensible fruitgrower from New Jersey, perhaps, or a middle-aged truck driver, who'd treat them decently and not cause trouble, but they wouldn't go for the nervous young men.

Bannion got the bartender's eye. "I'm looking for a girl named Lucy who works here. Is she around?"

"What's on your mind, friend?" The bartender was a large, middle-aged man with a narrow head and slightly protruding eyes.

"I just told you," Bannion said. He smiled because he never liked to play it tough. "Police business. Is she around?"

"Oh! Oh, sure. She's down at the end of the bar, this side, last stool."

"Thanks."

There was a girl on the last stool, a small, slender girl in a black satin dress, with dark hair cut in bangs above a round, pretty face, and eyes that looked very tired, but still cheerful. There was something appealing in her expression—some attractive blend of boredom and weariness, and the capacity for surprise. She smiled as Bannion approached her, and most of the tiredness left her face. "You must be Mr. Bannion," she said.

"That's right."

"I'm sorry about disturbing you," she said, sliding off the stool. "Let's sit in a booth, okay? When the band starts playing you need megaphones here at the bar."

"Fine." Bannion followed her to the rear of the place and sat down facing her across a cigarette-burned, drink-ringed table. A waiter came over and Bannion ordered a scotch and soda. The girl shook her head. "Only when I'm working," she said to Bannion.

"You're a hostess here?"

"Well, that's putting it pretty fancy," Lucy Carroway said, and laughed. "I would take a cigarette, if you've got one."

"Sure." Bannion lit hers, lit his own, and dropped the match in the ashtray. "Okay. What's on your mind?"

"Well, as I said, it's about Tom." She put a newspaper clipping which she'd been holding in her hand on the table. Bannion saw that it was the story on Deery's suicide from the latest edition of the *Express*.

"Okay, what about him?" he said.

"The story's wrong," Lucy said, in a tone of uncertain, confused defiance. She looked straight into Bannion's eyes. "He wasn't worried about his health, like it says in the story."

Bannion studied the girl. She struck him as oddly earnest and reliable. "Well, what was he worried about then?" he asked.

"He wasn't worried about anything. He was never happier in his life."

"He told you that?"

"Yes."

"When?"

"Last week, just five days ago."

"I see." Bannion drew on his cigarette, considering this news. It was rather surprising, in its implications, in the light of what he knew of Tom Deery, and, more particularly, of his wife, Mary Ellen Deery. "Supposing you tell me how you happen to know Tom?" he said.

She looked away from him then, and glanced at her hands. "Well, that's kind of a long story, Mr. Bannion."

"It could be a long night. Let's have it."

"All right," she said, and sighed. "Well, it was a long time ago, back in nineteen forty-one, that I met him. He had a summer home in Atlantic City, and I was singing there in a club. I started out as a singer. I didn't get into this racket until my

agent finally told me I was heading strictly from nowhere as a
singer. Well, that's another story, I guess. Anyway, I met Tom
when he came in one night for a drink and stayed for the
show. One of my friends there knew him and introduced us. I
liked him right away. He was a nice guy, gentle, if you know
what I mean. And he was always worried because the world
wasn't good enough, and because people were such bastards.
Lots of times his wife didn't come over with him—she used to
go off on her own, to Miami, places like that, he told me.
Those times, when she wasn't around, I'd go out to Tom's
place after the show. We'd go swimming early in the morning,
and then lie around in the sun after breakfast.''

"It all sounds very pleasant," Bannion said. He tried to
sound non-committal, but there was a touch of sarcasm in his
voice.

Lucy Carroway shook her head. "No, no, you've got it all
wrong," she said. She looked miserable and badgered. "I
don't blame you. I know what it sounds like. A guy tom-
catting around while his wife's away. But it wasn't like that.
Not with him, anyway. Just forget about me in this thing.
Maybe that's the way to make you see it. Check me off as a
hustling babe. But he was different. He wasn't happy about
the way we had to do it. Oh, I was happy enough. I'd take him
on any terms and feel lucky. But he was married and couldn't
forget it. He thought we were doing something terrible.''

"He loved his wife?" Bannion said.

"No, but he felt responsible for her. That was his trouble.
That's what made him such a sweet guy. He felt responsible
for everybody, for me, for his wife, for all the crookedness in
the world. He couldn't just enjoy himself and let the world go
to hell. Anyway, his wife wouldn't give him a divorce. She did
everything she could to hang onto him, things most decent
women couldn't make themselves do. She told him she was
pregnant—before that she wouldn't give him any kids. And it
was a lie. She said she had a miscarriage, but that was a lie too.
Trust her not to risk her figure having a baby. But she made
Tom feel responsible for the whole thing—the whole damn
bunch of lies.''

"This was all in nineteen forty-one?" Bannion said.

She nodded. "That was the start of it and the end of it. I

knew I was on a one-way street. I wanted Tom, don't think I didn't, but I couldn't have him without hurting him, and I didn't want to do that. So I bowed out, and that was that."

"And you've survived," Bannion said, with a smile. "Now, let's get to the point. What makes you think this story about his health isn't on the level?"

Lucy met his eyes. "I talked to him last week, had dinner with him, as a matter of fact. It was the first time I'd seen him since Atlantic City. We just bumped into each other on Market Street about five in the evening. His wife had gone to Harrisburg to visit her sister, he said, and he asked me to have a drink with him. It drifted into dinner. He was in a wonderful mood, happy and gay. I'd never seen him that way before. He told me he'd never felt better in his life."

"Was he referring specifically to his health when he said that?"

"Well, I'm not sure," Lucy said. "No, he couldn't have been, because we didn't talk about his health. There was no reason to. He looked fine, and he said he felt wonderful."

"The phrase is a fairly general one," Bannion said. "People use it to express a state of mind, satisfaction with work, things like that."

"But that's not the only reason I think something is—well, funny," Lucy said. "Tom just wouldn't kill himself. Not the way he was feeling."

Bannion paused, and then shrugged. "Lucy, the fact is Tom did shoot himself. That's definite."

She shook her head slowly, but some of the conviction, the assurance had left her face. "It just doesn't seem right."

"Tell me this," Bannion said. "Did he seem worried about anything else. Did he say anything about finances, about the wife, something like that."

"No, he didn't, and that's funny, too," she said, in a slightly surprised voice. "I told you how worried he always was, how he was always stewing about things. Like he was to blame for things being in a mess. He felt responsible for everything, it seemed. You'd think he felt guilty about not being able to take care of all the trouble in the world." She watched Bannion, excited and eager. "But last week he was a different person. He was really happy. He felt good. Like he'd just done something to ease his conscience, make him stop feeling guilty. I could tell. That's why I know he wouldn't shoot himself."

"Still, Lucy, he did." He frowned slightly and lit another cigarette. "Perhaps this change you saw in him, this happiness, was a result of his coming to terms with the world, and seeing it for what it is, neither heaven nor hell in itself, but a place you live in and make the best of."

"Well, if that's what happened to him, why did he shoot himself?" Lucy said.

"I don't know, Lucy," Bannion said. "However, and I'm frankly guessing now, he might never have got rid of that feeling of guilt and responsibility. Underneath, it worked away on him until he thought the only way to destroy it was by destroying himself. Maybe Tom never changed; maybe he was just as upset and insecure last week as he was when you met him the first time."

"I don't think you're guessing right," Lucy said, uncertainly. "I don't know why, I can't put it in words, but Tom was happy, really happy, last week. It wasn't just an act. I know it wasn't."

Bannion shrugged. "And I know that he shot himself."

"I've wasted your time, haven't I?"

"No, of course not."

She rubbed her forehead. "You've been really nice about it. I'm sorry about dragging you out this way."

"Forget it. That's what cops are for. If there's anything strange about a suicide we want to know about it. Now, how about having a drink with me?"

She shrugged and smiled. "Okay, Mr. Bannion."

Fifteen minutes later Bannion was on his way home. The curving river drive was silent and deserted. He drove at a steady fifty-five. An hour wasted on a wild-goose chase, he was thinking, but not with rancor. And then the habits of years caused him to amend the sentence. Probably wasted, he decided, and snapped on the radio.

Three

THE NEXT AFTERNOON Bannion spent an hour on deskwork, checking the progress of the three cases which were currently being handled by his shift. Two of them were going to the Grand Jury in the morning and were strong enough for that test; the third was back from the Grand Jury with a True Bill but the D.A. wanted it strengthened, if possible, before it went to court. Bannion gave Carmody and Katz the D.A.'s memo, and told them to get working at it. Burke's Negro was looking better all the time. His alibi—he'd been in a poker game with friends—had got an unexpected boost from the beat cop who had stopped by to tell them to cut down the noise. The Negro's friends would fade away, Bannion knew, afraid of getting involved themselves, but a cop for the defense meant practically an automatic acquittal. The D.A. would scream if they tossed this one at him, Bannion thought with a smile. Also the man's record looked good. He was employed as a body-and-fender man around town, had never been in any trouble with the police, and his family were respectable people.

Burke came over and sat on the edge of Bannion's desk. He was grinning. "Up in the air like smoke," he said, nodding at the report on the Negro.

"This is good work," Bannion said.

"I felt industrious last night, so I looked into it," Burke said. "My own time, too."

22

"I'll bet," Bannion said.

"We've got the wrong guy, I guess," Burke said.

"Well, we can let the right one go, which is something," Bannion said. He glanced at his watch. "I'm going to take a ride. I'll be back around five or six."

"Everything okay with Deery?" Burke said, as Bannion got into his coat.

Bannion hesitated, then said: "Yes, he shot himself, if that's what you mean. Did you know him pretty well?"

"Fairly well."

"Did you know that he had a home in Atlantic City before the war?"

"Yes, I had a drink with him there once. Met him on the boardwalk, and he asked me to stop by later for cocktails."

"What kind of a place was it?"

"Pretty nice. A high-class sweep-out, you might call it."

They walked toward the door, their voices and expression casual. "How did that figure on a police clerk's salary?" Bannion said.

Burke shrugged. "Prices were lower those days."

"And so were salaries," Bannion said.

"Well, maybe he had some outside work. Keeping books for a small firm, clerking nights, something like that." Burke stopped at the counter and put an elbow on it. "Maybe he was lucky at cards," he said.

"Yeah, sure," Bannion said.

"I always heard he was okay," Burke said.

"So did I. Well, I'll see you later."

"Right, Sarge."

Bannion went to his car and drove out toward Tom Deery's home, crossing the Delaware River at Spruce Street and heading out to West Philadelphia. The afternoon was cold and dry, and darkened here by smoke drifting from the loco-motives at Thirtieth Street station. Bannion had thought quite a bit about Lucy Carroway's story. It didn't add up to very much, but it had to be checked. That was the essence of police work; checking everything. A cop had to investigate all the ob-vious details, ask all the obvious questions, plod about doing things that frequently seemed pointless and stupid. The man-in-the-street and the editorial writers on the papers could tell him a quicker way to do it, of course. They knew that such-and-such an angle was impossible, unlikely and foolish. They didn't have to check it; they just knew. But a cop couldn't afford these seemingly logical short-cuts. He had to do all the tedious, useless work, because occasionally the impossible, unlikely or foolish areas of investigation turned out to be the most profitable ones.

Bannion parked and went into the vestibule of Deery's building and punched the bell. There was a short wait and then the inner door-lock clicked, and he went up the stairs to the first floor landing. Mrs. Deery opened the door. She seemed surprised to see him, but she smiled, and said, "Please come in, Mr. Bannion."

"I'm sorry to be bothering you again," he said, following her into the living room.

"I know it's necessary, so please don't apologize. I've just been to see Tom," she said, sitting down on the brocaded sofa and crossing her pretty legs. She was as flawlessly turned out as she'd been the day before, Bannion noticed. Her silver-streaked hair was done perfectly, her make-up was fresh and her manner was serene. Again he was impressed by the certainty and control of her manner. "He looks extremely well, I think," she went on. "And I must say everyone in the Department has been wonderful to me. The Superintendent called twice and there was a car here this morning, from the Mayor's office, I believe, to take me to the parlor."

"Well, that's only as it should be," Bannion said. He paused to mark a transition, then said: "I'm here on a different sort of business. I hope you'll realize this is my job, Mrs. Deery, and cooperate with me if possible."

"Why, certainly, Mr. Bannion." She wet her lip. "I'll help you in any way I can."

"Thanks. Last night I had a call from a woman named Lucy Carroway. Does that name mean anything to you?"

Mrs. Deery didn't change expression. She merely raised her delicate eyebrows, but it was enough to relegate Lucy Carroway into the realms of the unpleasant and unnecessary. "Yes, she was a friend of Tom's. Quite some time ago, I believe."

"She told me a very strange story," Bannion said. "She was positive there was nothing wrong with your husband's health.

She saw him last week, she said, and he told her he was feeling fine."

Mrs. Deery smiled pleasantly. "That woman is a liar, Mr. Bannion. Tom hadn't seen her for years, and most certainly not last week."

"Lucy said it was the night you were in Harrisburg," Bannion said. "Did you go to Harrisburg last week?"

"Yes, I did," Mrs. Deery said slowly. "I was in Harrisburg last Thursday night. Perhaps they did meet after all. That would be typical of her, of course. The instant my back was turned she—"

"She insisted it was an accidental meeting," Bannion said.

"Oh, I'm sure of that," Mrs. Deery said. Her slim hands trembled slightly. "I suppose she told you about her relationship with my husband."

"She wasn't very specific about it."

"What taste she's developed," Mrs. Deery said, with a little laugh. "She's obviously turned into a very fine lady." Mrs. Deery squared her slim shoulders and sat up a little straighter. "Well, it seems to be my word against hers, doesn't it?"

"No, of course not," Bannion said. "You must realize that we check things like this, even though we're certain in advance that they're preposterous."

"Yes, I understand," Mrs. Deery said, in a more reasonable voice. "I'll try to help you. I don't know if this Lucy Carroway and my husband were sleeping together. I presume they were. That's the chief appeal of women like that, I suppose. At any rate, the whole affair was so disgusting that I simply couldn't bring myself to care. I offered Tom a divorce, I made plans to divorce him, actually, but he came to his senses. I was younger then, but I decided it was all you could expect from a man. I took him back and it was a wise move, one I've never regretted. Tom has always been as loyal and devoted a husband as any woman could expect to find."

"I'm sure of that," Bannion said. He noted the discrepancies between Lucy's and Mrs. Deery's account of the affair, but on the whole, he thought Mrs. Deery's was probably closer to the truth. "Lucy said he seemed very happy when she met him last week," he said. "He had been worried, she said, when she first knew him."

"Undoubtedly," Mrs. Deery said. "Lucy's the sort who causes men to worry. That didn't occur to her, I imagine."

"No, I'm sure it wouldn't," Bannion said. He decided to nudge Mrs. Deery gently. "I had the impression she had something else on her mind, something she wasn't telling me. Can you think of any information, or fantasies, she might be holding back?"

Mrs. Deery shook her head slowly. "No, I can't. Would you mind telling me why you're interested in her story?"

"Of course not. If she's lying, and that seems obvious, I'd like to know why. She may be planning something which we can put a stop to if we have an idea what it is. It might occur to her to blackmail you for instance, with the threat of dirtying up your husband's name. She wouldn't have a chance, but people get funny ideas sometimes."

"That would be her type," Mrs. Deery said.

"Did you know her in Atlantic City, by the way?"

"I met her there just once."

"Well—" Bannion paused, then smiled. "Thanks again, Mrs. Deery. I'm sorry to bother you under these circumstances. But if Lucy tries to make any trouble for you just let us know. We'll put a stop to it fast."

"Thank you, I will."

They walked together to the front door. "This weather makes Atlantic City seem like a good idea," Bannion said. "Do you still have your place there?"

"No, we had to sell it years ago," Mrs. Deery said. "With the prices up, we just couldn't afford it."

Bannion nodded sympathetically. He thanked her again, shook her slim, cool hand, and went down the stairs and out to his car. In his opinion, the Lucy Carroway business was over. He rather regretted having forced Mrs. Deery back to what must have been a painful episode in her marriage—but that was his job.

At the office Bannion was caught in a sudden flurry of work. There was a fatal stabbing in the Nineteenth, and the body of a young girl had been found in Fairmont Park. The girl, a high school senior, had been beaten to death. She had been missing from her home since the night before, after breaking a date with her steady boy friend. Bannion sent

Burke on the stabbing, which was a routine job, and took Katz with him out to Fairmont Park. Each paper had three or four men on the job, and the Superintendent was making statements and having his picture taken. Bannion went at it carefully and slowly, nodding politely to the Superintendent's demands for an immediate arrest, and trying to keep the reporters out of his hair. This sort of job, the dirtiest and unhappiest in the book, Bannion thought, had to be broken the first day, even the first few hours, or it might drag on forever. Jerry Furnham, the tough, amiable *Express* man, finally gave him a worthwhile tip. He tapped Bannion's arm and said, "The boy friend, the one she stood up. He's all broken up, but he looked like he was crying before he got here. I saw him when he showed. Maybe he's got a crystal ball."

Bannion glanced casually at the young man, the girl's boy friend, a well set-up lad with a crew cut, and college numerals on his pull-over sweater. He was holding the arm of the girl's father, sobbing hysterically. Bannion rubbed his forehead tiredly. "Thanks, Jerry," he said.

He didn't get back to the office until two. The midnight-to-eight shift was on hand; Neely, Burke, and Carmody had gone.

"Long night," Sergeant Heineman said. "Don't forget to put in over-time, Dave."

"I won't," Bannion said.

"Tough about the kid in Fairmont Park," Heineman said. "The boy friend, eh?"

"Tough is right," Bannion said. "He fell apart before we got to him. He said he slapped her once, after the usual argument, and then got scared and knocked her around." Bannion shook his head. "He kept saying he was a clean boy. Well, Katz is still with him out in the District. They'll keep him there tonight, so you won't have to worry about him."

"I'd like an hour alone with that bastard," one of the men said.

Bannion sighed. "Take it easy, I'll see you around," he said to the room in general, and walked.

When he reached home it was a quarter of three. He was very tired, but he knew he wouldn't sleep if he went to bed. The business of the night, the bitter, meaningless heartbreak

of it, rested on his spirit like a pall. He sat down without
removing his overcoat and snapped on the light beside his
chair. For a minute or so he sat there, head resting against the
back of the chair, and then he took a slim, leather-bound
volume from his bookcase and let it fall open in his big hands.
He began reading at random, forcing himself at first, but
gradually slipping completely into the world of the well-
remembered words, a world that seemed a great and gentle
distance from the bitter one in which he lived and worked. It
was the *Ascent of Mount Carmel,* he was reading, the dark,
beautiful record of St. John's idealistic assumption with his
God. The words as much as the sense of it got through to Bannion. *"—Oh happy chance!—In darkness and concealment,
My house being now at rest . . . Oh night that guided me . . .
Oh night that joined Beloved with lover . . ."*

Bannion put the book aside fifteen or twenty minutes later,
and got to his feet. He stretched tremendously, feeling relaxed
and at peace with himself now, and then snapped off the
reading light and walked quietly through the dark hallway to
the bedroom.

Kate was asleep but she woke and switched on the night
light as he got into bed a few minutes later. "It was a long day,
wasn't it?" she said, and her voice was soft and warm with
sleep.

"Yes, pretty long," he said, resting his head on her
shoulder. "Put out the light, baby."

"Dave, you had a call. From a girl."

"Any name?"

"No, it was a gal I think. She said she'd leave the twenty
dollars she owed you with the bartender at the Triangle. That
was all. Are you in the small loan business, darling?"

Bannion got up on one elbow. "This isn't exactly funny,"
he said. He stared into the darkness, aware of the beat of his
heart, of Kate's soft nearness, the warm, comfortable silence.

"I'm sorry, I just took the message," Kate said.

"Well, I'll check it tomorrow," Bannion said, and put his
head down on her shoulder. They were silent a moment. He
said, "Would you lend me twenty bucks, baby, if I were cold
and hungry?"

"Sure."

*   *   *

There was work waiting for him the next afternoon and it wasn't until six o'clock that he was able to check into the phone call.

The girl who'd called had mentioned the Triangle—the only part of the message which made any sense. It was probably Lucy trying, for some reason, to get in touch with him without leaving her name. He signalled for an outside line and dialed the number of the bar.

"A man's voice answered: "Yeah?"

"This is Sergeant Bannion, Homicide Bureau. I want to talk to Lucy Carroway."

"Lucy? She ain't here any more."

"When did she leave?"

"Damned if I know, Sergeant. She was gone when I came on at three this afternoon. Maybe the boss could tell you, but he ain't around now, either."

"Okay, I'll stop by your place," Bannion said. "If your boss comes in, tell him to wait for me. Got that?"

"Yeah, sure thing. Say, what's up? Is she in some kind of trouble?"

Bannion put the phone down without answering and picked up his coat. The bartender's question echoed his own: *Is she in some kind of trouble?* That's what he planned to find out. She might have simply drifted on to another job, another city, but for some reason that didn't strike him as likely.

"I'm taking a ride," he said to Neely. "I'll be back in an hour or so."

"The lieutenant wants to see you," Neely said. "He's got someone with him now but said he'd see you in about fifteen minutes."

Bannion paced up and down the dusty, cigarette-littered floor, a faint frown on his normally good-humored face. "What's on his mind?" he said.

Neely shrugged, his reddened, terrier's face impassive.

Bannion walked to the window and looked down Market Street, dark now and jammed with hurrying pedestrians, hearing the faint, angry tooting of police whistles, the muted roars of traffic, looking at but hardly seeing the clean, beautiful height of the PSFS building, the huge Adam's clothes sign, the bright rows of store fronts flanking the dark river of the street. He finally glanced at his watch. "Neely, tell him I'd already gone out."

"But I told him you were here. He called while you were on the outside line," Neely said.

"Okay, tell him I was on something that wouldn't wait. I'll see him when I get back."

Neely shrugged, removing himself from the matter. "Okay," he said.

Bannion didn't bother with his car; in this traffic it would be quicker to walk. He reached the Triangle in ten minutes. The bar was almost empty now, the bandstand deserted, and only a few men sitting over beers. A show was going on next door; he could hear the sound of faint, emphatically syncopated music through the walls.

The bartender was the one he'd seen the night before. He came down to Bannion smiling. "Mr. Lewis ain't back yet, Sergeant, but he might be next door at the show," he said.

"Is there anyone here who can go over there with me and pick him out?"

"Yeah, sure." The man turned his head and shouted: "Jimmy! Hey, Jimmy! Come out here."

A thin, young Negro wearing a white apron pushed through a swinging door at the end of the bar, and glanced uncertainly from the bartender to Bannion. "Jimmy can show you," the bartender said. "Take the sergeant next door and pick out Mr. Lewis for him, Jimmy."

"Sure, just come along with me, please."

Bannion followed him into the street and into the lobby of the burlesque house. He showed his badge to the ticket-taker, and went into the dark, smoky theater. It was not a pleasant place; the carpets were worn and dusty, and the acrid tang of a urinal disinfectant seeped under the smell of stale tobacco and perspiration. The audience was a small one, fifty or sixty men crowded down in the first half dozen rows, but they were having a good time, laughing gustily at the pair of comics and the big, half-naked blonde on the stage.

The Negro, with Bannion following him, went down the side aisle on the left side of the theater, and called softly to a man sitting in the second row. "Gentleman here to see you, Mr. Lewis."

Mr. Lewis was slumped down so far that his head was almost out of sight. He was enjoying the show immensely; there were tears of laughter in the corners of his eyes as he looked over his shoulder. "What is it?" he said in an impatient whisper.

"Police business, let's step outside," Bannion said.

Mr. Lewis, a small, slender man, came to his feet as if a spring had been released underneath him. He rubbed both hands over his thinning black hair. "Sure thing, sure thing," he said, taking Bannion's arm. "You with the Liquor Control Board?"

"No, it's not that," Bannion said.

"Well, that's good news," Mr. Lewis said, laughing, following Bannion at a half-trot into the lobby. Bannion thanked the boy who smiled and left. Mr. Lewis was a sharply dressed little man, twitching with energy; standing still he gave the impression that he might break into a fast-jig-step. "Well, what is it, officer?" he said, slapping Bannion on both arms with open hands. "Damn, you're a big one, aren't you? Nothing wrong with the joint, is there, officer?"

"No, I'm here about a girl named Lucy Carroway. I understand she's gone. I want you to tell me about it."

Lewis looked relieved. "Why sure, sure. It was just last night. Right out of the blue she says she wants to be paid off. Well, they don't owe me nothing but a night's work, that's what I say. So I says, 'Okay, okay, Lucy, if that's the way you want it, the best of luck to you.' I paid her off and she left. Just like that."

"What time was it? Give it to me in order, as nearly as you can."

"Okay, I'll try." Lewis narrowed his eyes. "She went out for dinner at ten-fifteen, ten-thirty, something like that. It was after she got back that she told me about quitting, so that would be around eleven-thirty."

"Was she alone when she left and came back?"

"Honest to God, I don't know. She was alone when she talked to me about quitting. 'Mr. Lewis I'm quitting,' she said, 'and I want you to pay me off.' 'Where are you going?' I ask. 'South,' she says. How about that?" Lewis said, emphasizing the question by stamping sharply on the floor with an Adlerized foot. "Me, the fat-tailed money-bags, so they say, stuck here while a little bird like Lucy flys South. Capitalism, you can have it, I say frequently. Well, I paid her off, and off she goes. That's all I know. Is the kid in some trouble?"

"Not that I know of," Bannion said. "Where does she live?"

Lewis shrugged his shoulders and looked blank. "You got me! I should know, but I don't. You know, Inspector, them kids drift in and out like the tide. I mean, facts are facts, and most of them haven't got much more than a suitcase full of clothes between them and a charity ward. They drift, you know how it is. Nobody gives a damn about 'em, it's a fact. Lucy might be on her way to Miami and she might walk in tomorrow and want her job back. That's the way it is."

Bannion nodded, frowning. Wind forced its way under the double doors of the lobby, squeezed through the sides, and churned dust and tobacco along the wooden floor, tugged insistently at the frayed corners of garish, girl-adorned posters. "Yes, that's the way it is," he said. "Did she have any friends here among the other girls who would know where she lives?"

"That's a thought," Lewis said, snapping his fingers. "We'll go next door and see Elsie. They were pretty close. She and Lucy were always clubby." He laughted, taking Bannion's arm. "If they weren't both nuts about me I'd swear they were queer as three dollar bills."

Elsie was a tall, friendly blonde, with deep purple hollows under her eyes. She knew where Lucy lived, or had lived: The Reale Hotel, on Spruce below Sixth.

"I hope she's not in trouble," she said. "Lucy is a nice kid."

"No, this is just routine," Bannion said.

"Ah, you guys always say that, whether it's arson or stealing an atom bomb," Elsie said dubiously. "Anyway, I hope you mean it this time."

"I do, really," Bannion said. "Thanks, Elsie."

Bannion took a cab to the Reale, a third-class hotel with a

bravely clean lobby. He explained who he was and what he
wanted to the desk clerk, a young man who wore horn-rimmed
glasses and had an alert, inquiring manner.

"Miss Carroway checked out last night, sir," he said. "I
was on duty and remember the time. It was twelve forty-five."

"Was she alone?"

"No, she was with a gentleman."

"I see." Bannion lit a cigarette as a tired-looking man in his
fifties got his key, asked without hope for mail, and went
slowly to the elevator. "I wish you'd tell me as much as you
can about him," Bannion said. "Did they come in together?
Start there and let me have it all."

"Very well." The clerk frowned slightly and pinched his
thin nose. "They did come in together. Miss Carroway asked
for her key and told me she was checking out and to have her
bill ready when she came down. The gentleman stood behind
her, about six feet away, I'd judge, but looking away from me
so that all I saw was his profile."

The clerk paused, and Bannion let him take his time. He
was a good witness, with an eye for details.

"Miss Carroway and the gentleman took the elevator up to
her room," the clerk said. "Normally, that's against our
rules, but in this case, since she was leaving, I thought,
well—" He shrugged slightly. "It's not the best hotel in the
world, but we do try to maintain certain standards. At any
rate, they were down within ten or fifteen minutes. Miss Carroway paid her bill, it was for only three days, and then she
left. I think the gentleman had a car because there's no trolley
on Spruce Street any more, and the nearest cab stand is almost
half a mile from here."

"She didn't make a phone call here?"

The clerk looked apologetic. "I'd forgotten that. Yes, just
before she left she used the public phone here in the lobby."

"What did her friend do while she made the call?"

"Let me see. He went with her to the booth and waited
there, I believe."

"Did she close the door of the booth?"

The clerk smiled helplessly. "I'm afraid I didn't notice. No,
wait a minute. It must have been open because I heard her
talking. It's funny how things come back to you, isn't it?"

"Yes, one thing suggests another. What did she say?"

"I wasn't listening, you understand. It—her voice, I mean—was just like a noise, like music in the background. But she did say something about twenty dollars. I don't know how that fitted into the conversation, however."

"Twenty dollars, eh?"

"Yes, that's right."

"Now, what did this fellow look like?"

"He was a big man," the clerk said thoughtfully. "Not as big as you are, but pretty big. He wore a camel's hair coat, and his hair, what I could see of it, looked dark. He had on a white fedora, you see. His complexion was dark, and he had a rather large nose. That's pretty general, I guess, but it's the best I can do."

"It's very good," Bannion said. "Thanks very much. Could you recognize a picture of the man?"

"I'm not sure."

"Okay, I may stop back one of these days. Thanks again."

Outside, Bannion turned his collar up against the wind and walked west on Spruce Street. It was a long hike back to the Hall, seven to Broad Street, and three more over to Market, but he could use the time to sort out what he'd learned. It wasn't much, actually; unless something else happened he was at a standstill. But Bannion had a curious feeling that something else was going to happen.

Four

AS BANNION ENTERED the Homicide Bureau Neely winked at him and nodded toward the door of Lieutenant Wilks' anteroom. "You've been paged on the quarter hour," he said.

"Damn, that's too bad," Bannion said, returning the wink. He tossed his hat and coat on a desk and walked into the Lieutenant's reception room, where a uniformed cop, assigned to duty as Wilks' secretary, was busy at a typewriter.

The cop said, "The Lieutenant's expecting you, Sarge, go right in."

"Thanks."

Wilks was seated behind his desk, a tall, sparely built man in his early fifties, looking very trim and fit in the tailored uniform he wore in preference to street clothes. The room was unpleasantly cold; Wilks believed in the austere, vigorous life and except on the worst days of winter his windows were always flung open. He was also a cold-bath and long-hike type. "Sit down, Dave," he said, nodding at the chair beside his desk. "You've got me in trouble, so let's get it straightened out." Wilks affected the manner of a martinet; he talked forcefully and briefly, although not always with point, and had cultivated a stern, uncompromising glare. He was a driver, fairly smart about police work, but more valuable to the department as a distinguished, confidence-evoking figurehead. Wilks was excellent at banquets, Rotary luncheons, and women's clubs; his ascetic, cold-nipped face, and his trim body, the result of diet, exercise and a good tailor, were enough to diminish any doubts about the efficiency of the police department. The role had more or less been wished on him; whether he enjoyed it, Bannion didn't know.

"Drekker's been raising Cain with me, so I'm going to pass it on, Dave," he said. "What the hell were you bothering Tom Deery's wife about?"

Bannion was undisturbed by Wilks' hard face, the stern, accusing glare. He was interested that Mrs. Deery had made some sort of complaint, and more interested that the Department was taking it so gravely. "It was just a routine matter, Lieutenant," he said.

"Well, it struck me as a pointless piece of work," Wilks said, snapping the words out sharply. "Where the hell's your judgment, Dave?"

Bannion shifted slightly in his chair. "You'd better listen a bit now," he said. He felt anger surging up in him, pounding for release. This had always been his cross, a violent, hair-trigger temper that tore the control away from his judgment and reason. He fought it down now, as he had fought it for years. Bannion permitted himself no excesses of anger; he refused to pander to his buried need for violence, for unmotivated destruction. Bannion was known as a kind man, a gentle man, but only he knew the effort it cost him to play that role.

Wilks frowned at his tone. He reacted in one of two ways to insubordination; either he blew his top, toweringly, majestically, or else he accepted the challenge as directed against the Department instead of himself, and adopted a winning, they're-all-a-bunch-of-asses manner. He chose the latter course now.

"Hell, you know how Drekker is, Dave," he said, relaxing slightly and smiling. "Fine House Sergeant material wasted as an Assistant Superintendent, I've always thought. Anyway, he's in a stew about this matter, so let's calm him down. Peace in the family, eh Dave? Now, what's the story?"

Bannion told him about Lucy Carroway, of her story on Tom Deery, and the fact that she had quit her job at the Triangle. When he finished, Wilks shrugged and raised his eyebrows. "Well, I'll be damned if I can see what the fuss is about," he said. "You checked this Carroway girl's story with Mrs. Deery, which was certainly your job. Now the girl has packed up and gone, and that would seem to end the matter. Right?"

"It seems that way," Bannion said. "I do think it's strange that she cleared out, though."

"Why? These B-girls are a migratory crop, you know. Another thing, she might have got scared after talking to you, and lit out. Maybe she thought of causing trouble and then lost her nerve. As for her story about Deery's health, it's her word against the wife's. And I'd take the wife's word on it, particularly since there was no funny angle about the suicide."

"Mrs. Deery must have squawked pretty loudly," Bannion said. "What was her pitch, by the way? When I talked to her, she was very cooperative, very willing to help. I wonder what changed her mind?"

"No, Drekker said she was pleasant enough," Wilks said. "Don't blame her for this. It's Drekker, that's my guess. She was just curious about it, and called him. Well, you know how he is. Thinks all cop's widows should be beatified on the notification of their husband's death. And it annoyed him to think we were bothering her." Wilks paused, and then smiled. "I'll calm him down, don't worry. But don't bother her any more."

Bannion wasn't sure about Wilks. Most cops were honest, of course; Wilks probably was, on a form bet. The big boys didn't have to buy up every cop in the city. A half dozen crooked cops, strategically placed, could nullify the work of a thousand honest ones. Maybe Wilks was in that unholy little group. Bannion wasn't sure; but he disliked men who had to give certain orders obliquely, and with a smile. Wilks was still smiling at him now, and his words hung in the air. *"Don't bother her, Dave!"* This was an order, of course. Was it just Drekker's tender sensibilities at work? An insignificant little man had shot himself, but because he was a cop, his wife mustn't be bothered by the normalities of a police investigation. That hardly made sense. To a schoolboy it might, but it didn't to Bannion. *"Don't bother her, Dave!"* That was pressure. Where was it coming from? The big boys. You heard their names, you nodded to them on the street, and they had a police department, a whole city, in their hands. When they tightened the grip you could feel it.

"Okay, I won't bother her," Bannion said, at last.

"Fine," Wilks said, still smiling.

Outside he sat at his desk, ignoring the chatter in the room, staring out the dark window at the winking glare of Market Street. Finally he rolled a sheet of paper into his typewriter and wrote out a detailed description of Lucy Carroway. He read it over twice, frowning. It was okay, but he hesitated. At last he shrugged, walked over and handed it to Katz. "Take this up to Radio and tell him to put out a three-state alarm for her," he said.

"Okay," Katz said.

Bannion watched him leave the room, and then he sat down at his desk and stared out the window. He was sticking his neck out, of course; but so had Lucy Carroway . . .

He took time off the next day to make inquiries about a man with a big nose, dark complexion, black or brown hair, who might wear a camel's hair coat. The record room was no help; the description was too general. No one in the rackets detail knew the man, and he drew a blank at the detective districts scattered about the city. A numbers writer at Broad and Market looked startled and told him it sounded like his brother, who, he seemed relieved to add, was in Korea with the army. The only lead came from a plainclothes cop on the vice squad. "Could be a guy named Burrows, Biggie Burrows," the cop said. "Sounds like him, but your description is pretty vague. Anyway, Burrows is a Detroiter, came to work here for Stone just a few weeks ago. That's the talk. I don't know Burrows, just heard a few things."

"Burrows, eh? Well, thanks," Bannion said. He went back to the office, found things quiet, and went upstairs again to the record room. There was nothing on Biggie Burrows. Bannion told the sergeant to wire Detroit for their file on the man.

He checked Radio and drew another blank.

The three-state alarm on Lucy Carroway hadn't turned up a thing . . .

It was a quiet night. Bannion smoked and let his thoughts turn slowly, idly, in any direction they chose.

Biggie Burrows, in town for Stone. Stone was one of the big boys. The biggest in West. He could put on pressure. When Stone closed his hand, you felt it.

Carmody and Burke were arguing about politics.

"You got two parties, call 'em the Ins and Outs," Burke was saying as he paced the floor, an unusually serious expression on his long face. "The Ins have been in ever since we can remember. Everything is going their way. They account to nobody. That's how you get lousy government, bad schools, and hoodlums into a city. The politicians forget the city belongs to the people, and treat it like their own little cupcake."

"You think them Outs would do any better?" Carmody said.

"You're damn right I do," Burke said. "Not that they're better men in themselves, but a new broom does you know what. They'd come in, sweep out the drones, and chase the hoodlums under cover. In time they'd relax, of course, get just as bad as the old Ins. Then it's time to throw *them* out. That way you avoid these cosy, longterm contracts between the politicians and the hoodlums."

Bannion listened to them in spite of himself, in spite of Lucy Carroway and Biggie Burrows.

"Well, we'll see," Carmody said. "Elections are next month. We'll see what the people say about those Outs of yours."

"The people deserve their rulers," Katz said from behind his paper.

"What's that?" Carmody said.

"I read it in a book, so don't ask me what it means," Katz said.

The night stayed quiet, and Bannion smoked and looked out the window, thinking again of Lucy Carroway and what, if any, connection there could be between her and Max Stone. Tomorrow the shifts rotated and he would start on days for a week, working from eight till four. That meant a short night's sleep and he was glad that nothing came up to keep them overtime. Sergeant Heineman came in at eleven, an hour early, to give them that much of a break, and Bannion headed home, wondering when and if the three-state alarm would turn up

Lucy Carroway. If there was no news of her in the morning he'd have to forget about it, or send out an eight-state flyer—and he didn't have enough to justify that trouble and expense.

News of Lucy Carroway was waiting for him the next morning. Neely, who'd come in before him, handed him a report. "You were interested in this, weren't you, Dave?" he said.

Bannion put the carton of coffee he was carrying on the counter and took the form from Neely. He read it quickly.

The State Police at Radnor, Pennsylvania, had picked up a woman answering the description sent out the day before by the Philadelphia Homicide Bureau. Found on the Lancaster Pike at two o'clock in the morning by a passing truck driver, body of the deceased was presently at Saint Francis' Hospital.

Bannion rubbed his forehead slowly. *Deceased at Saint Francis.* He was aware of the smell of coffee beside him, of Neely's fragrant pipe, of the sunlight on the dusty floor, of all the sounds and impressions of the living world.

"I'm going out on this," he said to Neely. "I'll probably be back around noon. Keep an eye on things."

"Okay, Sarge," Neely said.

Bannion drove out along the Schuylkill, through Ardmore and Bryn Mawr, clean, pleasant Main Line villages with Packards and Buicks lining the street and housemaids doing the shopping in the business centers. The air was clear and fresh, and pale yellow sun brought the countryside to life, glinting in the river, gilding the gray Gothic heap of Villanova College, and making even the black winter woods seem warm and hospitable. It was vastly different from Philadelphia, Bannion thought. Here were first-rate schools, big homes, nice people.

What the hell had Lucy Carroway been doing out here?

Bannion turned off Lancaster Pike in Radnor and drove down an elm lined avenue to Saint Francis' Hospital. He walked into the tile-floored accident ward and told the nurse who he was and what he wanted.

"Yes, come with me, please," she said. She led him along a quiet, rubber-tiled corridor and stopped at a closed door. "Go right in," she said.

Bannion opened the door and entered a small carpeted

room, furnished with wicker chairs. There were flowers on a
table and three hunting prints on the wall. A tall, gray-haired
man stood up and put out his hand.

"I'm Parnell, County Detectives," he said. "You're Dave
Bannion, I guess."

"That's right."

"I saw your picture in the paper or something, I think,"
Parnell said. He had a thin, tanned face, and a high forehead.

There was a quality of lean, whip-cord toughness about
him. His hand was powerful in Bannion's, and his eyes were
those of a man who spent much of his time outdoors. "You're
interested in this girl we have here, eh?" he said.

"Yes, what happened to her?"

"She was pushed out of a car on the Pike sometime last
night or early this morning. Her neck was broken and her skull
fractured. She's in the next room now, the place we use as a
county morgue. I called for a Post and the doctor's ready to
go ahead. Let's go in."

"All right," Bannion said, removing his hat.

The unclothed body of Lucy Carroway lay on a long, zinc-
lined table, a table equipped with running water and built-up
sides. There was a powerful lamp above her, about two feet
from her body now, that could be raised or lowered from the
ceiling by a foot pedal. She looked very small, Bannion
thought, not much bigger than a child. The black bangs were
still neatly in place on her forehead. There was no expression
on her face; it was crumpled up like a piece of soiled white
cloth. He noticed details; the grotesque angle of her head in
relation to the shoulders, the smooth, cold look of her skin,
the tininess of her breasts, the rough abrasions on her hips,
legs and arms.

The coroner, a tired, earnest-looking man with a slight tic in
his left cheek, moved his foot and brought the lamp down
closer to her body. "See here," he said, glancing at Bannion
and the county detective. He pointed to spots on her slim legs,
a half-dozen of them between her ankles and knees. "Burns,
cigarette burns, I'd say," he said.

Parnell swore softly.

"Looks like it could be one of those upside-down sex
crimes," the doctor said, shaking his head. "There are rope

burns on her wrists and thighs. Maybe the fellow had his fun with her and then pushed her out of the car. You want her for something in Philly?''

"No, she was just—part of something else," Bannion said.
"Was she dead when she was pushed out of the car?"

"Can't tell yet," the doctor said. He tapped his scalpel on the metal edge of the table. "I'll know in fifteen, twenty minutes."

"Was she raped?" Bannion said.

"No, but as you know, you don't usually find that in cases like this. Well, I'll get started now."

Bannion walked into the next room with Parnell. He was damning himself bitterly, thinking, if I'd worked harder, moved faster, been smarter, maybe . . .

"What was your interest in her?" Parnell said, beginning to fill a short, black pipe. "This is my job now, and anything may help."

"Last week a Philadelphia cop committed suicide. Bad health, his wife said. Lucy Carroway said otherwise. She said he was in fine shape." Bannion shrugged and got out his cigarettes. "It wasn't much, you see, just a routine little funny business. Then Lucy disappeared. Now she's dead."

"That could be a coincidence," Parnell said. "My guess is she was killed by someone she met for the first time, someone who bought her a few drinks and took her for a ride."

"That could be," Bannion said.

The coroner joined them fifteen minutes later, wearing a tweed jacket and adjusting a dark red, wool-knit tie. "She was alive when she was thrown from the car, I'm quite sure," he said. "Death was caused, I'd say, by a splintered rib that went right through her heart. Of course, the broken neck, the skull fracture, either of those would have done it, too. But the rib went into her heart when she slammed onto the pavement. That's why I say she was alive when she went out of the car."

It seemed a moot point to Bannion.

He and Parnell went out to his car, turning up their coat collars against the wind. "Well, good luck," Bannion said.

"I'll need it," Parnell said. "There's a chance that one of our regulars can help us out. We know quite a few people who use the Pike at night. Newspapermen, some doctors, engineers for the power plants—they work nights and drive home late. We'll check all of them, see of any of them noticed a car parked on the road or anything else funny. Outside of that, we'll just have to pray."

"That's the way it is on some jobs."

"If you run into anything in Philadelphia give me a ring," Parnell said. "Wasn't anything funny about the cop's suicide, was there?"

"No, it was on the level," Bannion said. Parnell, he realized, was no dummy.

They shook hands and Bannion slipped behind the wheel of his car. Parnell sent his regards to some detectives he knew in Philadelphia. Then he said, again, "Let me know if you come across anything I can use."

"Certainly," Bannion said.

He drove back to the city, through the bright shining Main Line villages, disgusted with himself, and bitterly, savagely angry.

Bannion let the Bureau's work slide for a few days and dug into what he had on Lucy Carroway. The Detroit file on Biggie Burrows had come in, plus three pictures of the man. Burrows was a dark-haired, heavy-set hoodlum, who had averaged about an arrest a year, from Homicide to Assault and Battery, since emigrating to America from his native Sardinia twenty years ago. Real name: Antonio Burfarino. Bannion took the pictures to the clerk at the Reale Hotel, but the man couldn't make a positive identification.

"You see, he was wearing a hat, and never looked me full in the face," he said, studying the pictures of Biggie Burrows. In the police pictures, taken eight years ago, Burrows was hatless. "I—I just can't be sure."

"Okay, thanks."

Bannion began looking for Biggie Burrows then, through stoolies, bookmakers, numbers writers and prostitutes. He learned that Burrows had definitely been in the city, had been working for Stone, and had lived in a good, commercial hotel on Chestnut Street. But Burrows was gone now. Bannion went to the hotel he had been staying at and showed the desk clerks Burrows' pictures. They identified him positively. He had been with them for ten days, but had checked out without leaving a forwarding address. Burrows had checked out the same day that Lucy Carroway had dropped out of sight. There was a twenty-four-hour lag between the time she'd left the Triangle and the time of her death—in that interim she had been hidden away and tortured before being murdered. The set-up smacked of organization. No one can be kept for twenty-four hours against his will unless there are arrangements for a hide-out, money, food and transportation.

Bannion questioned everyone at the Triangle Bar, all the girls, the cooks, musicians, bartenders, and steady customers —but none of them had seen Lucy with a person matching Biggie Burrow's description. He wasn't discouraged, only impatient. He knew the break would come. One night he combed through the apartment houses near the Reale Hotel, checking one question with everybody. Had they seen a car parked before the Reale around twelve-thirty in the morning earlier in the week? Most of the people he talked to said they were in bed by that time, but a woman who happened to have been waiting up for a partying teen-age daughter remembered seeing a car in front of the Reale. She didn't know what kind it was, but it was long and shiny, and had a canvas top. Yes, a convertible, a big one.

That was pretty good, Bannion thought. Big convertibles weren't too common. Maybe Parnell, the county detective, might pin such a car down on the Pike. One of his "regulars" might have seen it.

He was working on the assumption that Biggie Burrows had murdered Lucy Carroway. It was an assumption he was ready to toss aside if anything else came along, but it was his best and only bet now. For one thing, if Lucy had been kidnaped, if Burrows had a gun on her while she was checking out of the Reale, then that afforded an explanation, a hypothesis at any rate, for her telephone call to him, and the mention of the twenty dollars.

Lucy, scared and in trouble, might have asked Burrows to let her make a casual phone call. She had tried to tip Bannion off, tried to point a finger at herself, by mentioning the Triangle Bar. It had been a desperate wave for help, but he hadn't seen it in time.

Bannion checked into Homicide on the third afternoon of

his hunt, feeling stale and tired. He signed the reports on his desk, said good-night to Neely, and walked over to the Y on Arch Street. There, in sweat clothes, he spent an hour working with weights—the only exercise that seemed to give his big body the physical release it needed. Three or four high school boys stopped to watch him. He stood solidly, feet well spread, and pressed a hundred-and-seventy-five-pound barbell above the head ten times in succession, and then, using two-minute rest periods, repeated the sequence five straight times. Bannion's body was like an engine; he could hook it to a job and it would run all day. He was no body-lover, no beach athlete. He felt an impersonal regard for his strength, as if he were merely a steward whose job was to keep it functioning at par. Bannion had learned that the more able a man is to stop trouble, the less of it he is likely to meet. And he didn't want trouble, he didn't want to use his hands on people. When circumstances forced him to, or when his temper jerked him out of control, he inevitably felt disgusted with himself and degraded. He knew the wild streak inside him and had tamed it, or frustrated it rather, by being strong enough to stop trouble before it started. It wasn't a unique problem, he knew; it was the problem of all the gentle giants in the world.

He put a towel around his damp neck and grinned at the boys. "That's the price I pay for liking potatoes too well," he said. He talked with them for a while, answered questions, showed them how to lift a barbell without risking a broken wrist, and then went down for his shower, feeling comfortably relaxed, the staleness gone from his body. He drove home thinking about dinner.

He was an hour late getting to the Bureau the next morning; he had stopped at a bar where some of Stone's men hung out to see if he could pick up anything on Burrows. It was a wasted trip. When he walked around the counter Neely pointed to Wilks' door. "Urgent," he said. "Very, very urgent."

"Well, well. Excited?"

Neely nodded.

Bannion walked into Wilks' office without bothering to take off his topcoat. Wilks looked up at him, then down at a report he was reading. "Take a chair, Dave," he said. He read for a moment or so, and then pushed the report away and looked directly at Bannion. "What are you working on, Dave?"

"Some angles on that Carroway girl's murder," Bannion said.

"That's a county job, isn't it?"

"That's right."

"Well, drop it, and get back to our business," Wilks said. There was flat finality in his voice. "You're not paid to do their work. I hope this doesn't come as a surprise to you, Bannion."

Bannion held his temper down. "Lucy Carroway, I think, was kidnaped and tortured in Philadelphia, then murdered in the county. I'm working on the first two ends of the job."

"That's not what you're paid for either," Wilks said, slapping his open hand sharply on the desk. "You're paid to run a shift, keep reports current and in order. Any man in the Bureau can handle the Carroway job. Do you think we made you a sergeant of Detectives so you can waste your time interviewing B-girls and hotel clerks?"

Bannion kept his mouth shut. The fact that Wilks had checked on him, or had been informed on him, was the most interesting thing he'd learned so far. He shrugged and let a smile touch his lips. "Okay, I'll pass it on to one of the boys," he said. "But I don't understand all the fuss. I just took a little time off to check some leads on this girl's murder. I was doing pretty well, too."

Wilks smiled, too. "That doesn't surprise me, Dave. I don't think there's any doubt that you can make a thorough investigation. The thing is, I want you doing the more important work, supervising your shift. Understand?"

"Sure, sure," Bannion said. "By the way, you remember who this Carroway girl is, don't you? She's the one who knew Tom Deery, who said his wife was lying about his bad health."

"Yes, I remember her," Wilks said. He looked at Bannion, then at his desk top. "I don't see any connection between that and her death, however. She was killed by a damn, misbegotten sex maniac."

"Yes, that's what the county man thinks," Bannion said.

"It's their job, remember that," Wilks said, returning to his executive manner.

"Who should I turn the Carroway job over to?" Bannion said. "Burke?"

Wilks hesitated for a few seconds. Then he said, in a casual voice, "Write a full report on it, and let me have it, Dave. I'll give it to someone on Heineman's shift. Your boys are busy enough, I think."

Bannion looked at Wilks steadily for a moment. "All right," he said, and walked out of the office.

Five

BANNION SAT AT his desk for an hour writing his report on Lucy Carroway, trying to calm himself with routine. This wasn't the first time he'd been jerked off a case; but it never happened in so raw and naked a fashion. Lucy Carroway's death had caused a rumble in the city. The heat was on, the fix was in, call it what you like. Bannion had been nosing around something safe and protected, ignoring the No Trespassing signs, and so to hell with honest police work, to hell with a murdered girl, keep away from it, Bannion. He couldn't guess why; but he knew who had the clout to stop an investigation cold. Stone, maybe Lagana himself. They were the big boys, the men with the big fists. But why? *Why*, in God's name? Why were they tightening the grip on behalf of Biggie Burrows, a two-bit mug from Detroit?

Bannion finished the report and put it in an envelope marked for Wilks. He knew it was a waste of time. This report was going to get so badly lost it would take bloodhounds to find it. He told Neely he'd be upstairs in Inspector Cranston's office if anyone wanted him, and started for the door. Carmody and Katz were playing cards, Burke was looking at a paper, and the room was quiet. Their faces were overly casual as they watched Bannion leave, and they said nothing when he had gone. They knew their big sergeant had been butting in where he wasn't wanted and had got his hand slapped. The

news traveled by what might seem like telepathy to an out-
sider; no one talked about it or discussed it, but the word
seeped and spread through the department. Everyone knew
Bannion had been looking for Biggie Burrows; and they knew,
again telepathically, that at this particular moment there was a
mile-high No Trespassing sign around Biggie Burrows. They
didn't talk about these signs, they walked around them, ig-
nored them, saved their energy for other jobs.

Bannion took one of the slow, bird-cage elevators up to the
fifth floor, and walked along the wide high corridor past the
Press Room, the now-empty Center-City Magistrate's court,
and turned into Cranston's office.

Cranston was nominally in charge of all police functions
in the Hall, responsible for records, filing-systems, radio and
communications. It was a do-nothing job, a sunshine detail, a
good spot for a drone or a trouble-maker. Cranston was no
drone. He was all cop, in the best sense of the word, a tough,
erect old man with hard, wind-roughened features, thick white
hair, and very clear, very direct blue eyes. Cranston was in the
Hall, on a sunshine detail, because he caused too much trouble
when he was out in the city. As a beat cop he had become a
legend by breaking up gambling parties in the Republican and
Democratic ward clubs, and on one occasion had hauled in a
top political boss and two Magistrates who had told him to go
away and mind his own business. At the hearing, a joke of
an affair since no Magistrate was going to commit a political
leader and two brother Magistrates on a gambling charge,
Cranston was treated as if he were on trial. His testimony, his
eyewitness evidence was smiled at, and his stupidity frowned
on; but he hadn't been intimidated. Asked why he had arrested the men, a silly question since the charge was on paper
at the Magistrate's elbow, Cranston had snapped: "They were
breaking the law!" The papers had liked that reply and played
up Cranston as a curiosity, if not as a hero, who rather sur-
prisingly arrested lawbreakers regardless of their political
connections. Successive administrations hadn't been able to
ignore Cranston. He was too tough, too smart, too respected.
He forced his way up, never compromising his own rigid standards. As a Captain he ran a clean district, as an Inspector, in
West, he had chased Max Stone back to Center City, and as

Acting Superintendent, a job he'd held only two weeks, he closed every gambling joint in the city, prepared indictments against Stone, and Lagana himself, and ran practically every gambler, pool-seller, and numbers writer across the river into Jersey. This was a little strong so Cranston went back to Inspector, and was assigned the sunshine detail in the Hall, where all he could do was ride herd on the paper work of the department.

He was at his clean, uncluttered desk, glancing through a police manual, when Bannion came in. "Hello, Dave," he said, smiling his brief, warm smile. "Don't tell me Homicide needs an old man's advice."

"Homicide's okay, but I'm not," Bannion said.

"What's the trouble?"

Bannion told him of the leads he had on Burrows, all of it, and that Wilks had jerked him off the case. "So, I'm mad," he said. "I'd like to turn in my badge and tell them inelegantly what they can do with it."

"So?" Cranston said. He fired up his pipe carefully. Then he said, "That's a decision a man must make for himself, Dave. Personally, I've stuck it out because a good cop can help the city. If things should change, I might be able to help still more. That's my choice. You've got to make your own. But I'll tell you one thing; if the situation in this town changes lots of people may have their eye on you." He smiled slightly. "They're willing to forget that you went to Notre Dame instead of Penn, Dave. Eventually, in fifty or sixty years, they may even forget that you made All-America there by knocking the daylights out of Eastern teams." He nodded, not smiling any more, and his old face was tough and hard. "They forget a lot in favor of an honest man, remember that."

Bannion shrugged. "I don't like working with the hope that someday things may change," he said. "That doesn't help me now. I don't like compromising, I don't like——"

"Hold on a minute. I've never compromised. I've done the job until they made me stop. Then I waited until I could tackle it again. Someday they won't stop me, they won't be able to, and that's the day I'm praying for."

"That's the future again," Bannion said.

"Okay, let's forget the future. Let's look at the present.

This deal of yours is sour. Deery kills himself. Start there. His wife says he was in bad health, the late Lucy Carroway says the opposite. Now if that's all there was, I'd be inclined to trust the wife. I'd write Lucy off as mistaken, over-emotional, or a liar. But she got killed after talking to you, and possibly by a mug working for Max Stone. That brings the thieves into it, and the picture changes." He smiled without humor. "I enjoy calling 'em thieves, you know. That's all they are. They'd rather think of themselves as racketmen, gangsters, mobsters, but they're just thieves to me. Well, anyway. You get a lead on Burrows, and then get taken off the job. Maybe somebody goosed Wilks. Maybe he did it on his own. So why are they worried about Biggie Burrows and Lucy Carroway? Why was she killed? Was it because she came to you with a story about Deery's health?"

Bannion shrugged. "I've got no answers."

"Well, we're back to Deery. Was that on the level? No chance he might have been bumped off?"

"No, that was on the level."

"And that is where things get screwy," Cranston said, shaking the stem of his pipe at Bannion. "Well, what are you going to do now?"

"I'll stick along," Bannion said. "I want to see the end of this business."

Cranston came to the door with him and patted his shoulder. "Remember this, Dave. Like they say about the British, or used to anyway, the people lose all the battles but the last one. Believe me, it works that way."

"Let's hope so," Bannion said. "Thanks, Inspector."

"Drop in anytime."

He met Jerry Furnham in the corridor. The reporter walked along with him toward the elevators.

"Everything quiet?" Furnham said.

"Nothing doing at all."

"Good. How about the Carroway girl?"

"That's a county job, Jerry."

"Yeah, but she voted locally," Furnham said. He smiled and looked sideways at Bannion. "That's why we're interested. The *Express* feels awful when a reader gets killed. We don't have that many to spare, you know." They stopped at

the elevators and stood there a few seconds in silence. Furnham was no longer smiling. It was raining again, the water
sluicing down the dirty windows of the Hall, blackening the
gray walls of the building.

"I thought you were working on this end of it," Furnham
said. "You off it?"

"Yes, I'm off it."

"Who's working on it?"

"You might ask Wilks."

Furnham pursed his lips. "That's an idea," he said mildly.
There was now a hard but patient line around his mouth. He
took out his cigarettes. "Smoke, Dave?"

"No thanks."

"Dave, the sex-fiend theory looks to me like a cover-up,"
he said.

"You're going to play detective now, eh?"

"What the hell are you sore about?" Furnham said. "I've
played ball with you, Dave. Now something stinks. I want to
know about it. I know the start. I know about Biggie Burrows,
for one thing. But I'm still curious, and I don't like being
treated like a dummy."

"You don't, eh?" Bannion said. He stared at Furnham,
suddenly transferring to him the anger he felt for Wilks.
"Then why don't you stop acting like one, Jerry? This is work
for the police department, not newsboys."

Furnham looked at him for a moment, and his face was
white under the blue smudge of his whiskers. "Okay, Dave, if
that's the way you want it," he said. He turned and walked
back along the corridor to the Press Room, his heels striking
the floor angrily.

Bannion felt sick of himself, sick of the lying and fencing.
He took a deep breath. "Jerry," he said.

Furnham stopped, turned around. Bannion walked to meet
him, rubbing his forehead slowly with one big hand. "I wish
you'd forget that, Jerry," he said.

"Oh, sure, just like that," Furnham said. He snapped his
fingers. "Nothing to it, Bannion."

"I mean it. I've got no right talking to you that way. Forget
it, will you?"

"Okay, consider it forgotten, Dave," he said, in a different voice. "Is that all you wanted to tell me?"

Bannion hesitated. "No, there's a little more. I had a good lead on Biggie Burrows. I think he's the man who picked up Lucy Carroway and murdered her. However, I just got that far before the case was taken out of my hands. Wilks has it now, and is going to give it to someone on Heineman's shift. That answer your questions?"

"Like hell he's giving it to Heineman's shift," Furnham said. He was smiling now, an odd little smile. "I talked to Wilks twenty minutes ago, Dave. This may interest you, by the way. Lieutenant Wilks said there was nothing to the angle you were working on that——" Furnham looked upwards expressively. "That, in short, it had gone up in the air. The stories don't fit together, do they?"

"Well, they're a little off at the edges," Bannion said dryly.

Furnham rubbed his hands. "Were you talking to me off the record?"

"Hell, no." Bannion snapped the words before he realized what he was saying. He was sick of cop-politics, of flinching when the big fists tightened their grip. "Do what you want with it, Jerry. You asked some questions, I answered them."

"You know, you sound a little like——" Furnham stopped and shrugged. "Well, be that as it may. Thanks, Dave. I'll see you around." He turned and walked quickly toward the Press Room.

Bannion went back and rang again for the elevator. He had missed a car by talking to Furnham, he realized. Too bad, too bad. It always cost you something to be honest, he thought, smiling faintly . . .

Furnham didn't use it as a news story because it wasn't one. He turned it over to the paper's political columnist, and it ran the next day, a sharp sarcastic item about certain differences of opinions in the Homicide Bureau. The difference stemmed, the writer hinted, from a clash over the amount of deference that should be extended to the city's hoodlums. They should be deferred to, of course; the argument was one of degree rather than kind. The Carroway murder was mentioned, and it was broadly suggested that a very likely suspect, a Detroit specimen, had practically been given a police escort out of town. The solution of the Carroway murder was held to be a highly dubious prospect so long as police investigations were hindered by political and hoodlum pressure.

It was a very strong piece of writing, stronger than the facts actually deserved, and it caused an uneasy rumble from top to bottom in the police department. Reformers come and go and are seldom noticed or missed. They shout their do-gooding strictures at women's clubs, at Boy Scout meetings, and once, in a very great while, they succeed in having a pool room closed, an extra traffic officer assigned to a school crossing, a known gambler arrested.

But a newspaper on a reform-binge is an altogether different matter. Papers know how to fight. They have seasoned men covering water boards, courts, police and fire departments, men who know all the nasty little secrets, who are, in short, an alert, intelligent, spy ring strategically circling the city. And the papers have a voice far louder than the do-gooder speaking at the women's clubs. It was the fear that those two things would be joined up, that the *Express*'s blast indicated a reform drive, that caused the rumble in the department.

Wilks raised hell about it, striding up and down his office, opening all the stops on his parade ground voice, but to Bannion the performance lacked the ring of honest anger. Underneath the bluster, the desk-pounding, the well-practiced glare, there was something hollow and anxious, something very much like fear.

"What business did you have giving him the story?" Wilks demanded for about the fifth time.

"Well, that was a mistake," Bannion said easily. "But what's everyone so excited for?"

"We don't want police problems aired in the papers," Wilks said. He paced the floor, glaring at Bannion. "You know that, for God's sake."

"Yes, but there's no problem really," Bannion said, in the same mild voice. "I wrote a report on what I'd learned on a case and passed it along to you. You said you were going to give it to someone on Heineman's shift." Bannion shrugged. "That's what I told Furnham. But he said you'd told him I was on a bum lead, that there was nothing to it. That's the point of confusion. Did you tell him that?"

"He misunderstood me, damn it," Wilks said. He smiled quickly and the effort put a white ring around his lips. "Dave, did you ever know one of those newsboys to get two consecutive facts down accurately?"

"They make a lot of mistakes, sure," Bannion said. He knew Wilks was lying, and it depressed him; the whole business was a stupid farce.

"But we're off the point," Wilks said. "You gave him the idea we're trying to cover up something here."

"Well, are we?" Bannion said. He was angry and disgusted, ready to force a moment of truth from Wilks. It would be better if they cut out this charade and spoke their minds.

"Of course not," Wilks said, slapping the desk with his hand. "What excuse do you have for letting him think we do?"

"Maybe I was just mad," Bannion said.

"You say 'maybe.' Were you, or not?"

"Yes, I was damn mad," Bannion said. "I was mad because I was getting closer to who killed Lucy Carroway, and that seemed to annoy someone."

Wilks looked steadily at Bannion. The silence between them lengthened, became oppressive. Finally, he said, "Let's don't be childish, Dave. You've got your orders, I've got mine. We do what we're told, and to hell with being mad, happy, bored or anything else. Let's don't have any more confusion on that point."

"I wasn't confused," Bannion said. "I was mad."

"Okay, okay, be mad," Wilks said in a fast, hard voice. "Be as mad as you want. Be mad at home, or in some pool room, but not around here. Things are run certain ways in this world, remember that. And they're run by certain people. You've always been above practical politics, haven't you? Well, that's a nice, high and mighty attitude, but it's unrealistic as hell." Wilks was pacing the floor, pounding one hand into the other with savage emphasis, and there was something in his face that surprised Bannion; it was a curious blend of envy and hate. "You read books about what life is like," he said, looking down at Bannion. "Well, get smart and throw them away. Look around you and you can see what it's like. It's not wrong or right, it's just the way things are. You'll learn that someday, Bannion. You'll see that you have to play ball, make compromises.''

"Well, that's possible," Bannion said, after a slight pause.

"Damn it, we're not in Kindergarten any more," Wilks said, in a more reasonable voice. He sat down at his desk and studied Bannion with a small smile. "Remember what I told you: we both have our orders. Do you understand that?"

"Sure, I understand it."

"Well——" Wilks hesitated, and his face softened. "Well, that's all, I guess."

"I'll get back to work, then."

Outside Neely and Carmody were discussing the *Express* story, but they stopped talking when Bannion came out of Wilks' office. There was a strange little silence, a drawn-out interval of tension, and then Neely cleared his throat and said, "Well, we're getting famous here in Homicide, Dave. Who snooped out the story, do you know?"

"It was Furnham," Bannion said.

"Well, I'm damned."

"You can't trust any of them," Carmody said.

Burke came in around the counter smiling, smelling of whiskey and cloves, his face flushed with the cold. "I'm glad my talents were overlooked and I stayed a simple old detective," he said, winking at Bannion. "That way you keep out of the papers."

"It was Furnham's story," Neely said.

"Damn them, they're always at some keyhole," Carmody said. "Why in hell do we let 'em in here, anyway? What good do newspapers do? They just print stuff to cause trouble?"

"They shouldn't cover police at all, if you ask me," Neely said.

Bannion listened to the talk, frowning slightly. He didn't know where Burke stood; he suspected Burke had brains. But Neely and Carmody, and too many other cops, would stand solidly against Furnham, and in back of Wilks. The names didn't matter; it was the principle of sticking together, of rejecting criticism, of presenting a solid front to reports, to do-gooders, to any probing of sore spots in the department. But a No Trespassing sign around it; that was the way to handle cancer. Cops leaned to the strength, whether they were part of it or not, leaned toward men like Lagana and Stone, who could apply the big pressure. Most cops weren't crooks, but they had to keep a respectful eye on certain big crooks. That's the way things were.

Bannion grinned slightly. "I gave Furnham the story," he said. "He just passed it along."

There was another little silence. Neely and Carmody looked at him, digesting this, and then they both shrugged. Carmody picked up a paper and Neely turned back to his desk. Bannion could almost feel the wall of indifference they put up to him; they wanted no part of this, thanks all to hell. He was acting queerly, ignoring some basic cop-rules, and they wanted no part of it, thanks again.

Burke came over and sat on Bannion's desk. He grinned, his eyes thoughtful. "You know, Dave, I thought it was a nice little story. Had good suspense. Makes you wonder what's going to happen next."

"Yes, I guess it did," Bannion said, slowly. He drummed his fingers on the desk. "Let's get a cup of coffee, okay?"

"Sure, Dave."

Brigid, his four-year-old, dark-haired daughter, was playing blocks on the living-room floor when Bannion got home late that afternoon. She wanted no hug or kiss or stalls, just some help in finishing her castle. "Okay, okay, Bossy," Bannion said, and dropped his hat and coat on the sofa. He tried to add a block to the archway, but she pushed his hand aside, and said firmly, "No, you just *watch,* Daddy."

Kate came in smiling. "There's my big man," she said, kissing him on top of the head. She wore a fancy apron over one of her good dresses. "Company?" he said, patting her on the ankle.

"Yes, Al and Marg are coming over for dinner. You'd better take a shower and get a drink ready."

"Okay," Bannion said. He didn't feel very much like company. Even Al and Marg. Marg was Kate's sister, Al her brother-in-law. They were nice people, but he didn't feel like seeing any kind of people.

"What's the matter with you?" Kate said.

"Nothing, I guess. I'll be okay."

"No, no, talk to *me*, not Mommy," Brigid said.

"All right," Bannion said, ruffling her hair.

"Dave, is anything wrong?" Kate said. "You've seemed down the last few days."

"Oh, it's nothing serious."

"Is it a case?"

"I told you it's nothing."

"Well, you'd better use another tone if you expect me to believe you," Kate said.

"Okay, I'll bring home an affidavit tomorrow night," Bannion said, with an edge to his voice. He stared at the castle Brigid was building. It looked like City Hall, he thought. He sighed and glanced at Kate. "I'm sorry," he said.

"That's okay. I wish you'd tell me, though, if something is worrying you."

"It's just a general let-down. That's an occupational disease with cops, I guess. This is one of the bad moments. Something came up this past week, and I feel like——" He hesitated, forgetting what he meant to say, but feeling a strong sudden anger flowing through him as he thought of Lucy Carroway. Slowly, unaware of what he was doing, he raised his big fist and smashed it down on Brigid's castle, on the tiny jumble of blocks that had reminded him of City Hall. "That's what I feel like doing," he said bitterly.

Brigid began to weep. She scrambled to her feet and ran to her mother. "It was a mistake, Daddy made a mistake," Kate said, patting her gently. She raised her eyebrows at Bannion.

"I'm sorry, Bidge," Bannion said. He rubbed his forehead, feeling silly. "There was a fly on the castle and I tried to hit it."

"There was *not* a fly," Brigid sobbed.

Fortunately the phone rang. Kate scooped the child up, and said, "Oh, let's see who's calling us." Brigid stopped crying. "Can I talk?" she said.

"Sure, of course," Kate said, and hurried out of the room.

Bannion got up and loosened his tie. He was thinking about making himself a drink when Kate came back to the room.

"It's for you." She still carried Brigid.

"Who is it?"

"—I don't know."

Bannion glanced at her, puzzled by her tone. "What's the matter?"

"Nothing at all," she said, but her face was white.

Bannion walked back to the living room and picked up the phone. "This is Dave Bannion," he said.

"Bannion, the big man from Homicide, eh?" The voice was low, smooth, amused.

"Okay, what is it?"

"You're off the Carroway job, I understand," the voice went on, smooth, liquid, a current of amusement running under it. "Is that the right dope?"

There was no point in asking who was calling. Bannion said, "Keep talking."

"Sure, sure, big man. Well, since you're off the case it might be a good idea to keep your big, large mouth shut about it. Understand? It's a simple word. Shut. Remember it. If you forget——"

Bannion slammed the phone down. In the living room Kate was on her knees gathering Brigid's blocks.

"What did he say to you?" Bannion said.

"He asked for you, and then he said——" Kate looked up at him and shrugged. "You can fill in the four-letter words, I guess."

Bannion pounded his big fist into the palm of his hand and walked up and down the room, his anger growing swiftly, dangerously. Finally he stopped and scooped up his hat and coat.

"I'll try to be back for dinner, baby," he said.

Kate looked at him and knew better than to ask questions. "Don't be late, if you can help it, Dave. Don't spoil our party."

"It won't be our party that's spoiled, baby," he said, and walked out.

Six

Bannion drove out to the city limits, to the exclusive section of Germantown, a lovely rolling area of gentle slopes, twisting lanes, and comfortable homes set well back from the streets and surrounded with handsomely kept lawns and trees.

Mike Lagana lived out here, in a sixteen-room house with an English country tone to it. His home was boxed by six acres of land, impeccably cleaned and pruned by a Belgian gardener, and sat sturdily and prettily in the cup of a shallow green valley.

Bannion parked and climbed out of his car. He noticed the uniformed patrolman who stood at the walk leading to the house. The cop noticed him too; he strolled over, a big, middle-aged man with thoughtful ruddy features.

"Who'd you want to see?" he said in a pleasant voice.

Bannion showed his badge, and the cop smiled. "Okay, Sergeant."

"I can go in now? That's nice."

"Sure, go right on in," the cop said.

Bannion walked toward the house, and then stopped and glanced back at the cop. "How many men on this detail, by the way?"

"Three altogether. Two in the back, and one in the front."

"Twenty-four hours a day, I suppose."

"Uh huh. Nights there's four, though."

Bannion smiled. "That's ten cops a day to watch Mike Lagana. Roughly, about a hundred dollars of taxpayers' money. You like the detail?"

The cop shrugged. "I do what I'm told."

Bannion stared at him and a touch of color appeared in the cop's face. "Yes, we all do what we're told, I guess," Bannion said.

"That's right," the cop said, relaxing.

Bannion walked down the graveled lane to Lagana's home. He went up the steps and sounded a brass knocker against an oaken door. He waited there on the wide porch, listening to the humming stillness, watching the cold, pale, late-afternoon light on the oily green leaves of the bushes that were planted beside the steps.

A dark-haired, teen-aged girl opened the door. She was slim and pretty in a flannel skirt and cashmere sweater. There was a jingling junk bracelet on her left wrist. Another girl stood behind her, holding a tray of Cokes. They looked at Bannion politely, smiling, and then the girl with the Cokes giggled.

"Stop it, Janie," the dark-haired girl said, trying hard to keep her own face straight. "Hello, I'm Angela Lagana," she said to Bannion. "You must think we're crazy, but Janie's had the giggles all afternoon. Please come in."

"Thanks, I wanted to see your father."

"Okay, I'll tell him," Angela Lagana said.

The girl called Janie giggled as Bannion entered the large foyer. "Honestly," Angela said, in an exasperated voice, and gave her a despairing glance.

A door off the hall opened and Mike Lagana appeared, hands on his hips, grinning at his daughter and her friend. "You monkeys," he said. He was a small, slender man, with gray skin, blue-tinged along the jawline, wavy gray hair, and a neat, black mustache. Mike Lagana looked as if he might be a capable, prosperous druggist. There was nothing remarkable about him physically, except his extremely good clothes, and his eyes, which were deep brown, and totally lacking in warmth, interest or any other expression. They might have been highly polished glass balls inserted in his narrow, commonplace face.

"What's all the commotion?" he said, smiling at the girls and Bannion.

"My name's Bannion, I'm with Homicide," Bannion said.

"A pleasure," Lagana said, extending his hand. "Okay, kids, beat it now."

The girls trotted up a flight of wide curving stairs, and Lagana smiled after them, his head cocked slightly, a soft little grin on his face. Their excited, conspiratorial rush of conversation was cut off by the sound of a closed door. Lagana laughed, glancing at Bannion. "They say kids keep you young, but I don't know," he said. "Come on in and sit down. What was the name again? I'm sorry, but I missed it."

"Bannion."

"Sure, I've heard of you," Lagana said, touching Bannion's arm and guiding him into a large, comfortably furnished study. There were deep chairs, a fireplace, a desk that looked as if it were used, and a pleasing view through French windows of gardens and trees. The wide mantel was crowded with portraits of Lagana's wife and children, and there was a picture of Lagana taken much earlier, as a young man, in fact, standing between a rather sullen-looking elderly couple in cheap, heavy clothes. Above the mantel hung an oil painting of a white-haired woman with a dark complexion and mild, worried eyes.

"That's my mother," Lagana said, smiling. "A great old woman. They don't make 'em like that anymore, eh? Our old mothers were the last of their kind." Lagana smiled into his mother's mild, slightly worried eyes. "Yes, a great old person," he said. "She died a year ago in May. She lived here with me, had her own suite, bathroom, everything. Well, that isn't what you came out for, I'm sure," he said, with a little laugh. "What is it this time? The Benefit ball game? Pension Fund drive?"

"I'm here about a murder," Bannion said.

Lagana looked surprised. "Yes? Go on."

"I thought you might help me on it," Bannion said.

Lagana seemed irritated now, but puzzled. "Who do you work for, by the way? Wilks?"

"Yes, Wilks. I'm here about a girl named Lucy Carroway, who was murdered last week. She was tortured first, then

tossed out of a car on the Lancaster Pike. It was an old-fashioned liquidation, and I thought—''

Lagana cut him off with a sharp, angry gesture. ''I don't
care what you thought. You've got no business coming here,
and you know it.'' He frowned at Bannion. ''I'm glad to help
you boys when I can, but I've got an office for that sort of
thing. This is my home, and I won't have dirt tracked into it.
We'll forget it this time, but don't ever make this mistake
again. Do you understand?''

''I thought you might help me on this job,'' Bannion said.

''Damn it, don't you hear good?'' Lagana said, in an angry
voice. ''Where do you think you are? A station house, or a
pool room, maybe? This is where I live, where my family lives,
where my mother died. What makes you think I want cops
stinking it up?'' He paused, breathing hard. ''I'm sorry to talk
this way. I don't like to. But you're out of line, friend, way
out of line. I said I'd forget it, and I mean it. This time. Now,
I'm kind of busy, so you'll have to run along.'' He put a hand
on Bannion's arm, and his expression changed; he smiled.
''No hard feelings, eh? Tell you what: See me downtown
tomorrow if you need some help. That's fair enough?''

Bannion returned his smile. ''I need help tonight,'' he said.

Lagana studied Bannion, frowning slightly. He seemed to
be making an effort to memorize every line in the detective's
face. Then he said: ''Okay, so you're stubborn. What's on
your mind?''

''A girl named Lucy Carroway was murdered,'' Bannion
said. ''I think she was killed by a man working for Max Stone.
A man from Detroit named Biggie Burrows. To start with, I
want him. And I intend to get him. I said before it was an old-
style liquidation, brazen and brutal. You don't want that sort
of thing in town anymore than I do. It might interfere with the
nice, quiet way things are running. That's why I'm hoping
you'll help me.''

''Is that all?''

''No, there's one other thing. I got a call this afternoon
—from one of your boys, I think. He told me to keep my
mouth shut about this deal. That annoyed me, Lagana. That's
why I came out here, which as we both know, is a foolish place
for me to come. But I want action. I'm stymied at the office,

so I'm trying you. How about it? Do I get some help?"

"What makes you think this man Burrows killed the girl?"

"Several things."

"You're not saying, eh? Well, you're a fool," Lagana said. "I told you twice I'd forget this but I won't say it again. You won't get another chance, friend." He paced the floor, staring at Bannion, a bright, angry touch of color in his gray cheeks. "I'll see that you don't make this mistake again, bright boy. I've met some prize dummies in my life, but you're in a class by yourself, Bannion. What's your trouble? You act like you're on the junk."

"You mean I must be crazy to violate your chaste, immaculate home," Bannion said slowly. "Is that it, Lagana?"

"Shut up, shut up, you hear," Lagana said. "I got nothing to say to you. Now get rolling."

"You think I must be taking dope, eh?" Bannion said, and his voice was deceptively soft. "Because I'm concerned about a girl's murder. She was no prize, perhaps, but she didn't deserve twenty-four hours of refined hell, and then a boot out of a speeding car. That bothers me and I want some help on it, and you assume I must be a dope." Bannion's voice grew louder, harder. "We don't talk about things like that in your home, eh? It's too elegant, too respectable, too clean. Cute little daughter, pictures of Mama on the wall. No place for murder, no place for a stinking cop. Just the place for a hoodlum who made his money and built this house out of twenty-five years of murder, extortion and corruption. That's what it is to me, Lagana. A thieve's temple. You couldn't plant enough flowers around to kill the stench."

"Bannion, you——"

"Shut up," Bannion said. "You're interested in homes, eh? Well, I'll tell you about some homes. Cops have homes. No places like this, but three and four-room apartments that run on a skin-tight budget. Sometimes those homes are empty as hell after the cop gets shot up, and sometimes there's no money at all if he gets hounded off the force by your men for trying to do a decent job. I've got a home myself, Lagana. Does that surprise you? Did you think I lived under a brick? Your creeps feel no compunction about phoning there, giving me orders, talking to my wife as if she were God's greatest slut. Cops have families, too, and even mothers. Decent people, most of them, living in a city with inferior schools, filthy parks, and rotten government, screwed by your hand-books, clipped by your numbers writers, and sickened by the kind of justice and order you've brought into their lives. Keep those people in mind, Lagana, when you're popping off about your own serene little corner of Heaven."

Lagana stared at Bannion, breathing hard. "Okay, okay," he said. "You've made your speech. I hope you'll think it was worth it, Bannion." He walked to his desk and punched a button beside a brass inkstand.

A man in a chauffeur's uniform appeared in the doorway, his eyes finding Lagana's alertly, questioningly. He was a big man with a pale, wide face, and the ridged forehead of a fighter. He moved easily, smoothly, his calf muscles bulging against black leather puttees, his shoulders straining the seams of his gray, whipcord uniform. "Yes, sir?" he said, in a gentle, incurious voice.

"George, take this character out of here," Lagana said. "Put him in his car."

The man turned easily, his big hand coming down on Bannion's forearm. "Let's go," he said, his wide, pale face impassive. "Take it easy," Bannion said. "I don't need any help."

"I said, let's go, friend," the chauffeur said. He pulled Bannion toward him with a powerful jerk, trying for a hammer-lock on the arm he was holding.

Bannion's temper gave, his control snapped. He straightened his arm, breaking the hammer-lock, and slammed George up against the wall. A framed picture of Lagana's daughter dropped to the floor at the impact.

"George!" Lagana shouted.

"Yes, sir," George said, in his gentle, incurious voice. He came out from the wall, watching Bannion carefully, thoughtfully. "All right, big boy," he said.

He feinted for Bannion's stomach with his left, then dropped his shoulder and brought his right over to the jaw. Bannion picked the punch off with his left hand, stepped in and slapped the man with all his strength across the face. It was a terrible blow; it sounded like a pistol shot in the room and George went down to his knees under it, shaking his head, his jaw hanging queerly.

"George, get him!" Lagana yelled.

George moved under the prod of that voice. He was bleeding now from the nose and mouth, but he crouched, got his feet under him, and looked up at Bannion. He stared into the detective's eyes, and a funny expression came over his face.

"Don't get up," Bannion said.

George wet his lips. "I'm not getting up," he said, his jaw wagging unnaturally with the word.

Bannion turned back to Lagana, and frowned. Lagana was sinking into the chair beside his desk, his mouth hanging open. He was breathing in slow, ragged gasps. His arm rose, his fingers fluttered at a table beside the fireplace. "The bottle," he said, rolling his head slowly, his shiny, expressionless eyes never leaving Bannion's face.

There was a tray on the fireplace table, and on it a small, unstoppered bottle and a glass of water.

"The bottle," Lagana said, in a low, pain-squeezed voice.

Bannion picked up the tray and put it on the desk within Lagana's reach. He watched Lagana pour a few drops from the bottle into the glass and then raise the glass slowly, jerkily to his lips.

"It's his heart," George said in the silence.

Bannion looked down at the man, who still crouched on the floor, the lower half of his face dark with blood. He felt an acute disgust for himself for causing that damage. "Well, that should be news to people who say he hasn't got one," he said. He looked at Lagana again, and then left the house and walked up the dark graveled path to his car.

The next night, about eleven o'clock, Bannion sat at home, an untouched drink beside him, smoking and staring at the ceiling. He was at a crossroads, and he knew it; either he went along and took orders, or he changed jobs. He had to keep his hands off Lucy Carroway's murder, or risk a head-on collision with Wilks, and the men behind him. That was the problem, all right. But did he have a free choice? Could he turn his back on Lucy's murder, smile and go on about something else? Or was he already committed? Bannion wasn't sure. He frowned, turning the question around in his mind, and sipped his drink.

The day had been uneventful; there had been no repercussions on his visit to Lagana. But the rumble in the department, in the city, was growing louder. The morning paper, the *Call-Bulletin,* had followed up the *Express*'s story with an editorial that asked a few pointed and critical questions.

"You're fine company tonight," Kate said, looking at him across her magazine.

"I'm sorry." He smiled at her, experiencing the same curious feeling of gratitude he'd had the night Tom Deery had commited suicide. "How about a nightcap?"

"No thanks." She suddenly raised a hand, and winked at him. "I think we've got a visitor. Brigid?" she called.

There was no answer.

Bannion grinned. "Come on in, baby," he said.

There was a rush of feet and Brigid appeared, blinking with sleep, and ready to laugh or cry depending on her parents' reaction.

"I can't sleep," she said, her head drooping, her voice and expression piteous.

"This is absolute nonsense," Kate said. "You just trot right back to bed, young lady."

She began crying and ran to her father's knee. He picked her up and she snuggled against him, looking triumphantly at her mother.

"According to the book this is the age where they have trouble sleeping," Bannion said. "The remedial treatment is to lead them back to bed with great kindness and firmness."

"Well, supposing you try it," Kate said.

Bannion sighed. "I walked right into that one, obviously. Okay. Bidge, would you like me to put you back in bed? You know everybody else is sleeping now. It's very late."

"All right," Brigid said, with a long sigh.

Bannion stood up, cradling her tiny bottom in the palm of his hand. "This is final, remember," he said. "No more hopping out of bed."

"You didn't put the car away," Kate said.

"I'll do my fatherly duty first."

Kate put her arm around his waist and gave him a hug.

"Well, if you're taking over my chores, I'll be a sport and put the car in."

"Thanks, but never mind. I'll do it."

"Oh, come on, I won't tear off a fender. Where are the keys?"

"You've never put it away, you'll knock the garage down."

"Well, we can chalk it up to experience. Where are the keys?"

"In my overcoat. But be careful, Kate."

"Oh, stop it, for Heaven's sake," she said. She got the keys, slipped a coat over her shoulders and went out. Bannion carried Brigid back to her room. He put her in bed, gave her the toys she wanted, and tucked the covers up around her neck. She stared up at him, her eyes bright with excitement.

"Tell me a story," she said, wriggling under the covers.

"Okay, but a quick one. A real quick one."

"Yes, a real quick one."

"Which one do you want?"

"About the pussy cat."

"Okay, the pussy cat it is."

There was an explosion in the street, a muffled, reverberating sound that shook the windows in the front of the house.

"Daddy, tell the story."

Bannion got slowly to his feet. "Just a minute," he said.

The echoes of the blast rolled away and in the silence he heard a man shouting in the street.

"Daddy, please tell the story," Brigid said crossly.

"Bidge, I've got to go outside a minute," he said. "You wait here, I'll be right back."

"But I—"

"Don't get out of that bed," Bannion said, and the sound of his voice made her begin crying.

Bannion left the room in long strides, ran down the hall and out the front door. Two men were trotting along the sidewalk, their heels sounding sharply in the cold, and across the street a window was being pushed up with a protesting shriek.

Bannion's car was before the house, under the shade of a tree. Smoke was pouring from it and the front end looked as if it had been flattened by a blow from a mighty fist. He leaped down the steps, his heart contracting with horror, and ran to the side of the car. The front door wouldn't open; it was jammed tight, buckled and wrinkled. Bannion smashed the glass with his fist, shouting to Kate in a wild voice. He got a hold on the door and jerked it open, pulled it completely away from the body of the car with a mighty, despairing wrench, not caring about, not even feeling the glass cutting into his hands.

There was no way to get her out; she was pinioned in the wreckage as if it were some medieval rack, but Bannion threw himself across her, shouting to her, and the sound of his voice, his insane, bellowing voice, halted the men who were running to the scene, brought pale, scared looks to their faces.

They crowded up behind him at last, seeing what he couldn't see; but it was a long time before they could get him away from her, make him realize that she was dead.

Seven

THE APARTMENT WAS clean and tidy, ashtrays emptied, newspapers and magazines in neat stacks, everything swept up, dusted, put in order. The flowers were gone, but their scent remained in the room, the faint, sickly smell of dying roses and lilies. Mrs. Weiss, who lived above the Bannions, had seen to these details the day after the funeral.

Bannion stood in the front room, his hands in his overcoat pockets, glancing about for the last time. There was nothing else to hold him here; Mrs. Weiss would take care of the subleasing, and of Kate's clothes. He dropped his keys on the coffee table, and then looked around again, at the imitation fireplace, the mantel, bare of pictures now, at the radio, liquor cabinet, at the sofa where she had usually sat to read, and at his own big chair. It was a room he had known by heart, but it was strange and unfamiliar to him now, as impersonal as a furniture arrangement in a shop window. It was a clean and silent room in a clean and silent apartment, and he looked at it without any feeling at all.

He glanced once at his books beside his chair, his old, familiar companions. He wasn't taking them with him, Hume, Locke, Kant, the men who had struggled and attacked the problems of living through all their lives. What could they tell him now of life? He knew the answers, and the knowledge was a dead, cold weight in his heart. Life was love; not love of

God, love of Humanity, love of Justice, but love of one other person. When that love was destroyed, you were dead, too.

The front bell rang. Bannion frowned slightly and went to the door. Father Masterson from Saint Gertrude's stood in the vestibule, a tall, earnest young man with pale skin and mild, unguarded blue eyes.

"Hello, Dave. I hope I'm not butting in."

"No, but I was just leaving," Bannion said.

"Well, I won't hold you up then," Father Masterson said. He turned his hat awkwardly in his big, gentle hands. "I just wanted to know if there's anything I can do."

"No, there's nothing you can do, Father."

"Do you mind if I come in for a minute?"

"No, of course not." Bannion stepped aside and closed the door, after the priest entered the room. Father Masterson glanced around nervously, and then turned to him with an earnest but hopeless expression on his face. "Talking's no good, Dave, and I know it. Some priests are good at it, but I'm not. When people say 'Why, why did God let this happen?' I just can't answer them. There's an answer, sure, and it's all right in catechisms, I guess, but not at times like this, times when you need it. Maybe I'm just no good, Dave. But—"

"I wouldn't worry about it, Father," Bannion said. He smiled slightly. He had changed in the last week; his face was thinner and pale, and his clothes hung loosely on his huge frame. His eyes were empty and expressionless. "I'm not asking for any answers. I know the answers. Perhaps we should reverse roles. I'll help you out, Father. Kate was killed because there was a stick of dynamite wired to the ignition of our car. When she stepped on the starter she was killed. Why was she killed? Someone was after me, and got her instead. That's all there is to it, Father."

"You can't live with this hatred in your heart," Father Masterson said, shaking his head slowly.

"I think it's all that's keeping me alive."

"What about Brigid?"

"She's okay. She's with Kate's sister. She thinks her mother is away on a trip."

"What are your plans?"

Bannion smiled. "I'm going to kill the men who put that bomb in the car, Father."

"You can't do that, Dave. Brigid needs you now, you've got to be father and mother to her. You can't do that with this hate in your heart."

"I think we've talked enough, Father," Bannion said. "We're wasting time."

Father Masterson was silent a moment, and then he smiled. "You know where I am if you need me," he said. "I'll do anything I can, remember that."

"You won't be any help to me," Bannion said.

Father Masterson hesitated. Then he said: "Dave, don't underestimate us. Sometimes, we seem to be offering a pretty timid sort of help. But there's more to it than that, believe me. Try to keep that in mind. And don't forget your little girl."

"I'll do what I can," Bannion said. "That's all any man can do. Right now, she's okay." He smiled again, the thin, humorless smile he had developed in the past week. "There's a police detail twenty-four hours a day at Kate's sister's home. The police aren't going to let this happen again. They're sorry it happened to Kate. So are the papers. Everybody's extremely sorry."

"There have been no arrests yet, have there?"

"No, curiously enough, there haven't. Curious, when you consider how sorry everyone is."

"Dave, justice will be done."

"Yes, of course," Bannion said, still smiling. "But I'll tell you a secret, Father. There won't be any arrests."

"You can't take that responsibility."

"Sure I can take it, Father," Bannion said. "Don't worry about that."

Father Masterson winced at the tone of Bannion's voice. He sighed and said, "Well, can I drop you somewhere, Dave. I have the car."

"No, thanks. I'll take a cab."

"Please, just a minute," Father Masterson said. "If you go this way I'm failing you, Dave."

"I haven't asked for anything, Father."

Father Masterson rubbed his forehead with long gentle fingers. "I know, I know," he said. "I—I feel useless anyway, though. You aren't taking your books, I see."

"No."

Father Masterson walked to the bookcase and peered at the titles. Bannion glanced at his watch, and then put both hands deep in his pockets. The priest removed a book from the shelf and came back to him holding it awkwardly, tentatively, in his hands. "Would you do me a favor, Dave? Would you take this one with you, please?"

Bannion glanced at it without expression. It was the *Ascent of Mount Carmel* by St. John of the Cross. "That's an interesting one," he said.

"You'll take it with you then?"

Bannion shrugged. "Let me read you something, Father," he said. He took the book and opened it, and there was a thin, unpleasant smile on his lips. "Listen to this, Father," he said, and began to read in an expressionless voice: "This light guided me. More surely than the light of noonday. To the place where he (well, I knew who!) was awaiting me—a place where none appeared."

Bannion closed the book slowly and looked at the priest. "Funny, isn't it?" he said.

"I don't understand, Dave," Father Masterson said.

" 'To a place where none appeared,' " Bannion repeated. "Maybe there wasn't anyone there, Father. Maybe there was never anyone waiting for us after the darkness of the night. That's a rather comical idea, don't you think?"

"That's not what he means," Father Masterson said.

Bannion shrugged again. "Well, I'm just quoting him, you know," he said. "If he meant something else, I think he might have said it."

"He did say it, he said it unmistakably in the last stanza of that poem," the priest said.

"I think I like the one I read better," Bannion said. "Come on, Father, let's go."

"But take the book, Dave," the priest insisted.

"Okay, okay," Bannion said, irritably.

They went outside and down the steps. It was a cold, raw day with a cutting wind in the black, winter trees. Father Masterson put out his hand. "Well, goodbye, Dave."

They shook hands. "Goodbye," Bannion said, and walked

down the street, his body inclined slightly into the winter-edged wind. He hailed a cab at the first intersection, and told the driver to take him to City Hall. He lit a cigarette and watched the gray, sluggish river, the low, leaden sky, and tried not to think. That had been the worst of it; thinking . . .

Neely was alone in Homicide, on the phone, and Bannion nodded to him and walked on into Wilks' office.

Wilks came around his desk quickly, his face concerned and anxious. "I didn't expect to see you yet, Dave," he said. He took Bannion's arm. "Here, sit down. Hell, we want you to take a complete rest, a good long one, before coming back to work."

Bannion didn't sit down. He watched Wilks.

Wilks coughed and took his hand from Bannion's arm. "We've got three men, full-time, on the job. There'll be a payoff soon, by God."

"That's good," Bannion said. "Nothing's turned up yet, eh?"

"Well, no. There's an angle——" He stopped, studying Bannion with an anxious little frown. "Dave, you don't want to talk about it now, I know."

"Sure, I'd like to talk about it," Bannion said. He smiled. "What's the angle?"

"It's this. There's a union official in your block, a fellow named Grogerty."

"I know him."

"Well, he's been in trouble with a left-wing outfit that's try-ing to crack one of his unions. We have some evidence that the bomb was meant for him, and not you, and certainly not your wife. His car was parked out that night, and it's a dark sedan, just like yours. We've been thinking the whole thing may have been a ghastly accident, a mistake."

"Oh, that's what you're thinking, eh?" Bannion said. He watched Wilks with the thin, unpleasant smile on his lips.

"Well, it's an angle. We aren't going to overlook anything, Dave."

"That's fine, neither am I."

Wilks paused. "How do you mean, Dave."

"I'm quitting."

"Quitting? Quitting what?"

"My job. I suppose there's a form to be filled out. I'll take care of it."

"Dave, slow down. What's the matter with you? Are you leaving town, or something?"

"No, I'll be around," Bannion said.

Wilks was silent a moment. "I see," he said, finally. "You're going to work on your own."

"That's right."

"I can't say that I blame you. I'd probably do the same thing myself. But this is a police job, remember that. Even though I understand your motives, and sympathize with them. I can't let you get in our way. Do you realize that?"

"Sure," Bannion said. "I'll try to keep out of your way."

"Dave, think this thing over carefully," Wilks said, rubbing his hands together nervously. "Amateurs get nowhere, you know that."

"I'm no amateur."

"Yes, but you can work faster in the department. Why don't you stick with us?"

"That doesn't seem to be the best way to get the man I want," Bannion said.

"Dave, I know what you're thinking."

"You should be worried then," Bannion said, in a suddenly cold voice.

Wilks stared at him and then walked around behind his desk, and put his hands on it, as if to draw some strength from that symbol of his position and authority. "I don't know what that crack means," he said. He seemed abruptly very tired. "What's on your mind, Dave?"

"I didn't come here to talk," Bannion said, with an impatient gesture. "I'll see you around, Wilks."

"Dave—you're making a mistake."

Bannion turned to the door.

"Dave, wait a minute!"

"Okay, what is it?"

Wilks swallowed hard and squared his shoulders. "I'll want your badge and gun, Dave," he said. His voice was crisp and solid with authority; but his eyes didn't quite meet Bannion's.

"The gun belongs to me," Bannion said.

"See that you get a permit to carry it," Wilks said.

Bannion smiled, took out his wallet and unpinned his badge. It was a special badge, a gold one, given to him by his shift on his tenth anniversary in the department. He glanced down at it, gleaming and yellow in the palm of his hand, and then he looked squarely at Wilks and closed his big hand slowly, powerfully, deliberately. "There it is," he said, opening his hand and tossing the badge onto Wilks' desk. It rolled onto the green blotter and came to rest on a neatly typed report, bent and curled as if it had been made of tinfoil.

Wilks wet his lips. "You'll regret that someday," he said slowly. "The frontpiece is clean, even if some of the men who wear it aren't. I—"

He was talking to the big detective's back. The door opened and closed, Bannion was gone. Wilks stared at his desk, at the crumpled badge, his lips still moving, finishing his sentence in a whisper. He stood there half a moment and then sat down and lifted the phone. "Outside line," he said.

He waited for the connection, dialed a number.

"This is Wilks," he said.——"Yes, I know what you told me, but this is important. Bannion was in. He's quit, going after things on his own." ——"I couldn't do anything with him." ——"I'm not worried." Wilks rubbed his forehead. "Sure, he's just a dumb cop." ——"Okay, okay." ——"All right."

Wilks replaced the phone slowly. There was a film of perspiration on his upper lip . . .

Bannion stopped in the outer office, at Neely's desk. Burke had come in and was lounging against the counter, watching Bannion with a small, worried frown.

"Neely, I'd like a favor," Bannion said.

"Sure, anything, Sarge."

"I want the names of any automobile mechanics in town who have police records. The districts should be able to get them for you."

"Sure, it won't take long."

"One thing, before you start. I'm not with the department anymore. I just quit."

Neely looked at him in surprise. "You're kidding?"

"No, that's on the level."

"For God's sake, Dave, I don't know what to say. That's classified information. I'm not supposed to pass it out."

"I said it was a favor."

"Dave—— I can't do it," Neely said, looking unhappily at his phone.

"Okay, sorry I asked," Bannion said, and started for the door. Burke straightened up from the counter, and said, "What the devil did you quit for, Dave?"

Bannion didn't answer. He straight-armed the swinging door, almost jarring it off its hinges, and turned out of sight into the corridor. Burke swore and went after him, half-running. He caught up with him and put a hand on his forearm.

"Don't go off your rocker," he said, in a low, tense voice. "Relax. I'll get those names for you, but take it easy. You want to take something apart now. I don't blame you—but be smart about it, boy, be smart."

They reached the elevators and Bannion faced Burke, his face hard and pale. "I'll be smart, don't worry," he said, and shook Burke's hand from his arm and stepped into the elevator.

The doors slid shut . . .

Burke walked slowly back to the Homicide office. He glanced at Neely as he rounded the counter, and shrugged. "What's up?" Neely said. "What's the matter with him?"

"I don't know," Burke said, shaking his head thoughtfully. "He's not using his head. But I wouldn't want to get in his way. I've seen him mad, and that's bad enough, God knows, but this is different. He's going off like a bomb, you watch."

"*You* watch," Neely said, reaching for the ringing phone. "I want no part of it."

Burke shrugged and lit another cigarette . . .

Bannion had to wait a few minutes in Inspector Cranston's outer office. When he did go in, Cranston stood and put both hands on his shoulders. "Is there anything at all I can do, Dave?" he said quietly.

"I'm here for a favor."

"You may have it. Nothing helps at times like these, least of all talk. But you must know how I feel."

"I think so. I've quit, Inspector. I want a permit for my gun."

"You're going to handle this yourself, eh?" Cranston said, after a pause. "Going gunning. That's against the law, Dave."

"So is leaving bombs in cars," Bannion said.

Cranston frowned and sighed. "Well, I'll skip the fatherly advice. You're no child. You know what you're doing. It will take a day for the permit. Where shall I send it?"

"I've moved into the Grand Hotel on Arch Street."

"Okay, I'll send it over by messenger in the morning. Is there anything else you need?"

"No, that's enough, Inspector."

Cranston rubbed his white head, still frowning. "Dave, let me ask you a favor now. Don't forget where my office is. Okay?"

Bannion nodded. "I'll remember," he said.

Cranston watched him leave. He sighed and took a gun-permit from his desk, and began filling it out, his hard old face expressionless.

Bannion walked to his hotel. There was a fine rain falling now, and the winter darkness was closing in on the city. Neon signs flashed above store fronts, and automobile headlights bored yellow tunnels into the gray, wet gloom. He picked up his key at the desk and went up to his room, which was neither large nor small, friendly or otherwise, but simply an impersonal, adequate hotel room. He poured himself a drink and sat down at the window without bothering to remove his hat or coat.

He stared at the city. Now it's time to start, he thought. It was a satisfying realization, it gave a purpose and outlet to the storm inside him.

He watched the city, a black, rain-shining mass, glittering with red and white lights, a cramped, crowded city, squeezing its densest glut of men and buildings into the corridor made by the hourglass curves of the Delaware and Schuylkill rivers. He watched the city, drinking.

Lots of people there. Most of them didn't give a damn about him, or about Lucy Carroway, or his wife. Some did though; bondsmen, racketeers, a few cops, magistrates, judges, sheriff's deputies—they cared about Bannion. They had to, whether they were for him or against him, whether they were straight or crooked, because the pressure had been big when it came, and everybody on a city payroll, everybody who made money out of the running of the city, had to care, had to worry when the big pressure was on, when the big hands tightened their grip.

Bannion finished his drink. He didn't kid himself; it would be a tough job.

He glanced at his watch.

Time to start.

He stood and checked his gun, and then slid it easily back into its holster. He took the copy of St. John of the Cross from his pocket, looked at it for an instant, and then tossed it onto the top of the bureau. He felt as if he were putting down an unwelcome burden.

He walked out.

Eight

THE WOMAN WAS middle-aged, with graying hair, wide, cautious eyes, and skin the color of milk chocolate. Bannion stood on the stone stoop of her house, the collar of his trench coat turned up about his throat against the rain.

"I'd like to talk to your son, Ashton," he said for the second time.

"He ain't home, he don't get home till seven most nights. What you want with him? He in trouble?"

"No, he's not in trouble. I just want to talk to him."

"You a policeman, ain't you?"

"No, I'm not."

The woman hesitated, looking up and down the dark rainy street anxiously, holding a sweater close about her neck with one strong hand. She glanced at Bannion, the caution and fear that was as much a part of her as her skin showing in her wide, brown eyes. "No use you drowning out there. Come on inside and wait for him."

"Thanks."

The house, an ace-deuce-trey type on Pine Street, with three rooms stacked one on top of the other, was shabbily furnished but clean. Bannion stood in the living room and the woman excused herself and went downstairs to the kitchen. There was a warm, pleasant smell of stewing meat and rice in the house. He didn't have long to wait. The front door opened, letting in

80

a gust of damp, cold air, and a man who wore overalls and a leather jacket. This was Ashton Williams, the young Negro Burke had had in two weeks before as a murder suspect.

He stopped and stared at Bannion, and then looked around quickly, confused, like a man coming into the wrong house by mistake. His big-knuckled hands played with the seams of his pants.

"What you want?" he said in a low voice.

"I want you to do me a favor," Bannion said.

Ashton scratched his head. "What you want?"

"My wife was killed last week. Maybe you read about it. Somebody put a bomb in my car, but she got it instead of me. I'm after the men who did it."

Ashton shifted his weight uneasily. "Why you come to me?"

"You've worked around garages as a body-and-fender-man. You know that car bombs aren't on sale in the five-and-ten. They've got to be put together, to order, with a detonator to attach to the ignition and a stick of dynamite. Honest mechanics don't make them. But someone did, someone who wasn't an honest mechanic. That's the man I'm looking for, Ashton."

"You come with trouble," Ashton said. "Squealing to the cops is trouble."

"I'm not a cop anymore," Bannion said. "I quit. You can tell me to go to hell if you like."

"Well, I'd sure like to," Ashton said, with an uneasy smile.

Bannion stared at him. "Is that your answer?"

"You treated me decent," Ashton said. "I don't know why, but you did. What you want me to do?"

"Do you know any mechanics in town who have police records?"

Ashton frowned and rubbed the side of his face. "Right off, I can't say. I heard once there's a fellow in Germantown who did eight years in Holmesburg, but I don't rightly know if that's true." He continued to rub his face. "There's a boy now, works in West Philadelphia, in a place on Woodland Avenue. I know him my own self, and he said he was 'rammy' once. That's prison talk, ain't it?"

Bannion nodded. "Means the D.T.'s. Tell you what, Ashton: Think it over tonight, try to remember anyone you've ever met who talked or acted as if he might have done time, and I'll check with you tomorrow. Is that okay?"

"Yeah, that's okay," Ashton said. "I'll do some askin', too."

"Well, be careful about that," Bannion said.

"Sure, I'll be careful." He came with Bannion to the door. "I hope you catch that man who put the bomb in your car."

"Thanks," Bannion said. He shook hands with Ashton and walked down the wet block to Fifteenth Street where he could catch a trolley to his hotel. It was too late now to go out to Al and Marg's; Brigid would be in bed. He didn't really want to see her; she'd ask about Mommy and he'd lie to her, knowing it was stupid, but lacking the guts to tell her Mommy wasn't ever coming back, ever.

There was an envelope from Burke waiting for him at the hotel desk, and it contained a list of eight names and addresses, mechanics with police records, now working around town. The man heading the list worked in a garage in the Northeast on Ruan Street. His name was Mike Greslac . . .

It took Bannion five days to run down the list, and he didn't get a lead. Six of the men had air-tight alibis, the kind they couldn't have bought or arranged. The seventh man was an alcoholic who couldn't remember where he'd been the night Kate was murdered, but Bannion didn't think it was likely that anyone would have hired him for a tricky, shady job. The man drank, and drunks talked. The last of the lot, a youngster with a pleasant wife, told him to go to hell. Bannion had expected more of that; working without a badge was tough. However, the youngster seemed straight, and Bannion put a question mark after his name. If nothing else turned up he'd see him again; and then he'd slap the truth out of him if necessary.

Burke gave him three more names, and in a note said that these completed the run-down on mechanics with records. Ashton turned in four names to him but two of them had been on Burke's first list. Bannion checked the new names he'd got from Burke with no success. He was back where he'd started. In a week he'd been in almost every garage in the city, had talked to every mechanic with police trouble in his past, and had learned nothing. He wasn't discouraged. The break would come. Something was always left lying around lose. You had to keep looking, keep checking, to find it. It took time, and he had time.

He decided to start working on the other end of the job, Mrs. Deery.

The weather had been cold and wet. Bannion's clothes needed attention so he sent three of his suits out to be cleaned and pressed, and gave the bellboy his laundry. He spent a couple of evenings at Al and Marg's, playing with Brigid before she went to bed. They had two kids a few years older than Brigid and she was excited and happy about staying with them. But she woke at night crying for her mother and had to be rocked back to sleep, Marg said.

She said they'd keep Brigid until Bannion decided what he wanted to do, regardless of how long that took, and Al, her husband, an earnest balding man who worked as an inspector for the Gas Company, was prepared to lend him a thousand dollars if he needed it. They were excellent people, Bannion realized, but he couldn't saddle them indefinitely with his troubles. He would have to make plans for Brigid—only after he had settled this job.

Inspector Cranston had sent him the gun-permit as he had promised he would, and Burke had insisted he use his car. Bannion didn't hesitate; he took the car immediately, instinctively, as he would take anything now that might help him find Kate's murderers.

He was ready to leave for Mrs. Deery's one morning when the phone in his room rang. It was Ashton.

"I heard about another fellow, Mr. Bannion," Ashton said. "Fellow name of Slim. That's all the name he got, I guess. He work out around the graveyard for the last couple months, but he's gone now."

"He had a record?"

"Yeah, he blew up some safes, I been told."

"Thanks, Ashton. I'll try to find him."

"I hope he's the one you want, Mr. Bannion."

"I do, too. Thanks again, Ashton."

The "graveyard" was a mile-long stretch of automobile junkyards in West Philadelphia that crawled like a rusty ugly growth along the border of the city. Dozens of offices, most of them unpainted shacks, dotted the area. The dealers here bought wrecks, cut them apart and re-sold the parts to small garages, and to individuals who repaired their own cars. Every yard had small mountains of bodies, democratic heaps of smashed-up Cadillacs, and broken rusty Fords, and rows of tires curling like thick gray snakes around the orderly stacks of fenders and wheels. There were bins of headlights, pistons, sparkplugs, and rows of drive shafts, rear ends, and brake drums, all price-marked and ready to be hauled off.

Bannion drove out to the graveyard in the morning, and spent the day tramping over the frozen, cinder-covered ground, and asking about a mechanic named Slim. He talked to laborers cutting up wrecks with torches, and to yard owners, who were usually in their shacks beside a coal stove, but none of them had any specific information. Some of them had heard about a man named Slim. "Maybe at some other yard," they said.

It was at practically the last yard that he got a lead. The shack had a sign above it, reading, *"Smitty's. Best Prices!"*, and inside was a young man poring over a list of penciled figures. He was big and solidly built, a blond with thick hair, a square, unshaved face, and very light, sharp eyes.

"Yeah, I knew a guy named Slim," he said, glancing up at Bannion. "What about him?"

"Do you know where I might get in touch with him?"

"You a cop?"

"No."

"Private cop? Insurance investigator?"

"No, just a citizen," Bannion said. "But I want to find this fellow Slim."

"Well, I got no reason to cover for him, but I ain't got time to answer a lot of questions," the blond said. "Don't get me wrong. You a cop, or something like that, it's one thing. But just private business I got no time for, understand."

"I'll try to make it short," Bannion said.

"I told you how I stand," the man said, getting up and facing Bannion. "I'm no information clerk, or something."

Bannion didn't want trouble; he couldn't afford it. But he wanted answers. "You don't seem very friendly," he said, putting his hands casually into his pockets. The lapels of his coat spread and the butt of his gun protruded a half inch or so, catching a gleam of light from the glow of the stove. The blond's eyes flicked to it and away quickly.

"Funny, you look friendly," Bannion said.

"Well, I'm not trying to be a hard guy," the blond said.

"No, of course not. You were just busy when I came in, a little short on time."

"Yeah," the blond said, and wet his lips.

"Well, you aren't so busy now," Bannion said. "Things have slacked off, it seems. When did Slim leave here?"

"About a week ago. Eight days it was, I think."

"What did he do here?"

"Worked around. You know. Tore the wrecks down, things like that."

"Was that all?"

"That's all he did for me. He did a job for some other guy though just before he left."

"What kind of a job was it?"

The blond young man looked into Bannion's eyes and something there brought a funny dryness to his throat. "I don't know, Mister," he said. "Honest. He took a day off to do it, that's all I know."

"Then he left here, eh?"

"That's right, he left."

"Where did he go?"

"I don't know. He told me once his home town was Chester, but I don't know if he went there or not."

"He left eight days ago," Bannion said, in a low voice. The time checked, he thought, feeling the anger beating in his temples with a sense of bitter pleasure.

"Who was the man he got this job from?" he said.

"I can't help you much there."

"Try," Bannion said.

The blond wet his lips. He was having a little trouble talking. "Well, you see, he parked out on the avenue and honked. Slim went out and talked to him. I guess they knew each other. The man in the car was well-dressed, I could see that much, and he looked, well, kind of tough."

"What kind of a car was it?"

"A Buick. A new one. A blue convertible."

"Thanks very much," Bannion said.

"Don't mention it. Glad to help."

Bannion walked out to Burke's car, and the big blond young man sat down and spent three matches lighting a cigarette. He got up and put a shovelful of coal on the glowing, pot-bellied stove. The place was cold all of a sudden, he was thinking, cold as a damn grave.

Bannion headed for Chester. He drove past the airport and out the Industrial Highway, past the mammoth Baldwin locomotive works, and the sprawling properties of Sun Oil and Shipping, keeping the speedometer needle brushing seventy. This might be the lead he was thinking, the loose end that was left around after even the neatest jobs. Once he got his hands on it and began pulling, the rest of it would come out into the light.

It was dark when he pulled up before police headquarters in Chester. The building was two-storied, of red brick blackened by generations of industrial smoke and soot. Bannion had been here before on cases, so he took the side entrance that led directly to the detective bureau on the second floor. There were three men in the single, high-ceilinged room, big redfaced men who looked the part of police officers in a tough, dirty town, built on oil, shipping and steel. Bannion knew one of the men, a detective named Sulkowski. They shook hands while the other two men looked at Bannion with interest. Sulkowski said awkwardly that it was tough, damn tough about his wife. They'd read about it, and knew he had resigned from the department.

"I don't blame you," Sulkowski said. "I'd go after the bastard on my own, too. I wouldn't let nobody rob me of the fun of getting the guy."

"Well, that's why I'm here," Bannion said. "Do you know a man from this area who's called Slim? He's an automobile mechanic when he's going straight, and a safe man when he's not."

"Slim Lowry," Sulkowski said. There was an odd silence in the room. Bannion caught the look that passed between the other two detectives.

"What's the matter?" he said.

"Slim was a pet of ours," Sulkowski said. "Spent more

time in jail than out." He looked unhappily at Bannion. "The thing is, Slim was a lunger, and he died day before yesterday. Damn, I'm sorry. Was it a good lead?"

"It could have been pretty good," Bannion said. "Was there anything funny about his death?"

"No, he died natural. Only funny thing was that he had damn near five hundred bucks on him, and was living with some shines over on Second Street. How would you figure that?"

"Did he die there?"

"No, in the hospital. The folks he was living with gave the boys downstairs a ring night before last, and they sent over the wagon. He died a couple of hours after they checked him into Chester General."

"What was the address of the people he was living with?"

"You want to see 'em, eh? I'll get it for you, don't worry." He turned to one of the detectives. "Call downstairs and get that address, Mike. Bannion, you want one of us to go along with you?"

"No, thanks. I can find the way."

"Damn, I hope you get what you want."

When the address came up, Bannion made a note of it, shook hands all around and went down to his car. He drove through the business section of the city to the slums, into streets of two-storied, yellow-brick tenements without central heating or interior plumbing. Colored children ran along the sidewalks, shouting shrilly at each other through the darkness. Bannion found the address he wanted, and knocked on the door. He heard footsteps, and then a latch clicked and a tall, strongly-built woman with a shawl over her shoulders was staring at him with narrow, unfriendly eyes.

"I'd like to talk to you a moment," Bannion said, removing his hat.

"What about?"

"A man named Slim Lowry. I understand he lived here with you."

"That's right. He's dead though, you know."

"Yes, I know. May I come in a minute?"

The woman looked undecided. "Come ahead," she said, at last, and walked back through an unlit hall to a living room in which a pot-bellied coal stove was burning. A man lay on a sofa in the shadows, an old man with white hair and blank, sightless eyes. He had a blanket over his legs and lay on his back staring at the ceiling. Occasionally he made a small coughing noise in his throat.

The woman sat on a straight chair near the stove and looked up at Bannion. "You a policeman?"

"No, a private citizen. Why did Slim Lowry come here?"

"He was a high-flyer, I guess. Liked the atmosphere of the place."

"You can help me if you will," Bannion said.

"I said he liked high living. Why go to a hotel when there's places like this around. Makes sense, doesn't it?"

"You've got no monopoly on trouble," Bannion said. "My wife was murdered last week. Blown to hell by a bomb someone put in our car. I'm trying to find out who did it. You could help if you will."

The woman was silent a moment, her eyes grudgingly going to the hat still held in his hand. "Well, that's too bad, Mister," she said in a changed voice. "Slim came here to find the place he used to live. This was a white neighborhood once, and he came back to his old house. He was sick, and in some kind of trouble, so I let him stay. He went off his rocker pretty regularly. Tried to chase us all out once. Said Papa there stole the place from his old man. Stuff like that. He was in real trouble, Mister."

"Did he have any visitors?"

The woman shook her head. "He talked about somebody who was coming. He kept saying he'd explain it wasn't his fault."

"Did he ever use the phone?"

"No."

"Get any calls?"

"Yeah, he got one. But that was the night he died. I'd already called the police, when this party called to speak to Slim. I told him Slim was sick, that he was going to the hospital."

"Do you know who it was who called?"

"Yeah, he gave a name. First I told him Slim couldn't come to the phone, see. He started cussing me then. Said, 'You tell him it's Larry Smith.' Then I told him Slim was damn near dead and was going to the hospital. So he hung up. Say, what's the matter with you? All you white people are nuts, I think."

"Larry Smith . . ."

Bannion stared at the woman, not seeing her, rubbing his big hands together slowly.

There was always a loose end in even the neatest jobs.

Here it was . . .

Nine

LARRY SMITH STOOD on Market Street at the corner of Twelfth, smoking a cigarette and smiling at the noise and color and excitement of the Saturday night crowd. He was a solidly built, well-dressed young man of twenty-six, with curly black hair, and a tough, knowing, handsome face.

A stocky seaman in a pea jacket came up alongside him, and said, "Hello, Mr. Smith. Didn't keep you waiting, I hope."

"No, I've been here just a few minutes," Larry said, smiling and flipping his cigarette out into the street.

The seaman needed a shave, and looked shaky and hungover. "I wish you could of seen me last night. Saved me a lousy head, I think."

"I was busy. Did you have any trouble?"

"Naw, it was simple. I got the stuff from a guy in Livorno who brought it down from Milan. I sailed from Genoa, landed here in Philly night before last. I brought it ashore in a cigar box, with my sewing kit and some letters on top of it. Three pounds of it, Mr. Smith. And now I need dough."

"I can't say for sure until I talk to the boss," Larry said.

"Hell, you told me to get it. Is this a stall? I can sell it to someone else, you know."

"No, you can't," Larry said, still smiling. "You got one customer in town. That's us. Remember that."

The seaman shrugged, his face sullen. "Okay, okay," he

90

said. "You'll get in touch with me tomorrow?"

"Yeah, I'll know by then for sure. Where you staying?"

The seaman gave him the name of a hotel on Market Street near the river. He said goodbye and walked off with a rolling gait, hands stuck disconsolately in his pockets.

Larry went briskly down the block to his car, a blue Buick convertible, which was parked under a No Parking sign. He climbed in, grinning at the cop on the corner. The cop grinned back and tossed him a cheerful salute. Larry was late, so he stepped on it; the date with Stone was for eight and it was damn near that now. He was picking up Stone at his automobile agency, and then they were going to Stone's apartment to meet Lagana. Lagana was boiling about something, Stone had said. The Bannion deal, probably. Well, there were always slip-ups. There wouldn't be another though, by God.

He headed for West Philadelphia, forgetting Bannion, thinking about his new deal. Lagana was against dope, he knew. The old man was worried about the loudmouth reformers. Larry wasn't; you always have them around, dogooders, busy-bodies, their pants in an uproar about slums, garbage collections, colored people being kept out of polling stations, gambling, all the rest of it. They were griped because they were on the outside. Give them a cigar with a bill under the tinfoil and they'd tip their hat and forget the reform stuff pretty fast. Now, he had the dope deal all set. Lagana would have to let him go ahead; the stuff was here, the buyers were lined up, and a steady supply was assured for the future. There was money in it, beautiful permanent money. Guys quit playing the horses if their wives griped enough, but they never quit the dope. The Horse, the boys called it. Larry smiled through the windshield, seeing and liking the reflection of his twelve dollar shirt, his strong teeth, his tough, handsome face. That was one horse they never quit playing, he thought, still smiling.

Max Stone was waiting for him on the sidewalk before his neon-shining, block-long automobile agency, a huge, red-faced man with small, irritable eyes. He was wrapped up in two hundred dollars worth of camel's hair coat, and there was a soft gray fedora on his large, round, balding head. Larry opened the front door and Stone got in beside him, puffing

with the effort, and twisted himself into a comfortable position in the leather-covered seat.

"You're late," he said. "What the hell kept you?"

"I had to see a guy," Larry said, releasing the clutch and
starting down Walnut Street under a rush of power.

"All right, all right, this ain't the Indianapolis Speedway,"
Stone said. He took out a cigar and fumbled at the wrapper.

"We're in a hurry, I thought," Larry said, grinning.

Stone grunted. He lit his cigar with a gold lighter and blew
smoke at the windshield. It didn't taste right, he thought.
Stone was a direct, blunt man who liked things he could taste,
smell, feel. He liked eating, drinking, wenching, good cars,
the track, poker games. He liked Jewish food, especially. Lox
and cream cheese, big Kosher pickles, matzoh ball soup, sour
red cabbage, pastrami, cheese cake. He gave that to the Jews;
they knew how to feed themselves. But his stomach was going
back on him: food like that burned him up, and a night of
drinking left him feeling like holy hell for a couple of days.
He'd be on toast and milk pretty soon, he thought, watching
the store fronts flash past, and a pedestrian leap back to the
curb, his face disappearing behind them in an angry frightened
blur.

"Damn it, slow up," he said. His temper, always near the
breaking point lately, suddenly snapped. "Do what I tell
you," he shouted.

"Okay, okay," Larry said.

"Well, that's better," Stone said.

"What's Lagana want?" Larry asked, as he slowed down in
the traffic approaching the Schuylkill river.

"He's bitched-off about the Bannion business," Stone said.
"You'd better let me do the talking tonight."

"I can do my own talking," Larry said. "What'd he want
me to do? Knock him off with a fly swatter?"

"Damned if I know," Stone said. "The thing is, you didn't
do the job, with or without a fly swatter. Let's wait until we
talk to him." He put the cigar back in his mouth, frowning.
Stone wasn't used to reflection; he preferred action. But he
knew there was something wrong, something queer in the city.
There was a feeling, a groundswell, and he didn't like it, didn't
understand it, and it made him mad. Things were out of line; a

cop or two, a few magistrates, even some of the big boys at the Hall. Stone thought it was time to slap down, and hard; but Lagana said no, and he meant it. Maybe the boss knew what he was doing, and maybe he was just getting old.

Larry parked on Walnut Street before Stone's tall, gray apartment building. He left the keys in the ignition and told the doorman to park the car. Stone walked into the quiet, carpeted lobby, moving characteristically fast, staring straight ahead, his head and shoulders inclined forward as if he were advancing to meet an enemy. He had the top two apartments in the building, the seven-room penthouse for business and entertaining, the space below for living quarters. The management was pleased with the arrangement; Stone's parties in the penthouse were insulated from the rest of the building. He was a valuable tenant; the management realized that when they got their tax bills from the city.

Stone and Larry took the elevator to the penthouse. Alex, Stone's cook-valet, a middle-aged man with a nervous smile, let them in and took their coats and hats.

"I'm having a poker game tonight," Stone told him, smoothing down his thinning hair. "We got plenty to drink?"

"Yes, there's plenty."

"Well, see that there's French Cognac. Judge McGraw is coming and he won't drink nothing else. You got money?"

Alex said no, smiling nervously.

Stone swore and gave him a bill. "You'd think I was feeding an army the way I pour dough into this joint," he said to Larry. He strolled into the big living room, annoyed with himself, and pointlessly angry at everything else. He wore a tan gabardine suit, with a white shirt and red tie. The clothes were expensive, but their effect was ruined by his pot belly, and hulky, rounded shoulders. He looked hot, rumpled and irritable. "Well, let's have a drink," he said. He glanced at his watch, and his eyes, imbedded in pouches of flesh, glinted with annoyance. "Mike's late. We break our tails getting here, so *he's* late."

"What'll it be?" Larry said.

"Scotch and plain water. Make it a double. I guess I need a lift." Stone walked to the French windows that opened on a terrace and stared down at the curving, shining river, and at

the lines of traffic on Chestnut and Walnut streets. This was
his city, he thought moodily. He could close his fist and make
it squirm. What the hell was wrong? It must be this lousy
cigar, he thought, turning away from the window. The room
was large, warm, softly lighted. It was expensively furnished,
with the best rugs, chairs, sofas, and tables on the market; but
there wasn't a personal touch in it. Stone liked it that way. His
idea of class was a suite in a good hotel. The decorator had
wanted to put in monk's cloth drapes, low, round coffee
tables, modern furniture, and even wall murals. One of the
murals was to have been a city skyline with a top-hatted
chorus line kicking their legs in front of it. Stone rubbed his
balding head and looked around the room. Once a guy got
money everybody tried to take him for a chump, he thought.

Larry brought him the drink. Stone took a long, appre-
ciative swallow. That was more like it. He needed to relax,
have some fun. To hell with worrying. What was there to
worry about, anyway?

"That you, Max?" a high voice called from the other end of
the apartment.

"Yeah, Larry's with me," he said.

A girl came in from the dining room, smiled at Larry, and
kissed Max on the cheek. He put an arm around her waist.
"What've you been doing all day?" he said.

"I shopped a little. Bought some shoes."

Stone put a hand to his forehead in mock alarm. "A little
shopping! I know what that means, Debby."

"What a man," Debby said. She grinned at Larry, who
shook his head sympathetically. "How about a drink?" she
said, patting Stone's cheek. "Can you afford that?"

"Sure. Fix her a drink, Larry."

Debby was a strikingly attractive blonde of twenty-seven or
twenty-eight, with a healthy, blooming complexion, the softly
rounded forehead of a baby, and serene blue eyes. She owned
and took excellent care of a tall, spectacular body; her waist-
line was almost tiny enough for Stone to encircle with his big
hands, and her legs were those of a dancer, long, slim, beautifully muscled.

Stone sipped his drink and watched her with a small,
unguarded smile. Something about her got to him, made him

feel oddly unsure of himself and shaky. She was wearing a gold lamé hostess gown that matched her hair perfectly, and high-heeled golden sandals on her feet.

"Thanks, pal," she said, smiling, and taking the drink from Larry. Debby's dispositon was one of her major charms. She was always in good spirits, happy and pleased with life, and as she put it, without the time to be tired or moody. Debby was no fool; she had worked for ten years before meeting Stone, as a maid, a waitress, a bar hostess, a dancer and model. Those jobs were tough and demanding. You got up early, earned your money, and it wasn't much, and went to bed dead-tired. It was a never-won battle against room rents, runs in stockings, making old clothes last and scrimping for a good hat twice a year. It was being nice to guys, but not too nice, and still getting in trouble in spite of your promises to yourself, and then having the bastards run out on you. Stack that up against living with Stone, and it was small wonder that she was happy. She had him right where she wanted him too. He thought he was a big man when he was with her, and that was a feeling he couldn't buy anywhere else for all his money. Stone was an old man who still had to think he was about nineteen in bed. He didn't understand himself or know what he needed, and she wouldn't tell him; but the knowledge put her in the saddle.

The buzzer sounded and Stone went to the door. Lagana came in, neatly dressed as always, and behind him his shadow, the big man called Gordon. Lagana unbuttoned his black, Chesterfield coat and rubbed his hands together briskly. He glanced around, smiling at Debby and Larry. "Well, how's everyone tonight?" he said. "Rather cold, isn't it?" He wore a banker's gray suit, and a conservative tie. His shoes were polished but not to a high gloss and the handkerchief in his breast pocket had been folded in a square so that no points showed, except for his eyes, he might have been taken for a prosperous druggist. Gordon drifted over to the fireplace and stood there, nodding to Larry. He was a big, awkward man who gave the impression he could move fast, if it became necessary.

"I'm sorry to be late," Lagana said. He smiled, his teeth white under the narrow black mustache. "My daughter was going out formal, if you can believe it, and she wanted me to wait and put the final okay on her dress. I told her it didn't matter what I thought—just impress that young football player who's paying for the corsage and dance bid." He smiled at Debby. "Was that good advice would you say?"

"Somtimes the old man means more than these football players," Debby said. She knew Lagana was a sucker for his kids. "They come and go but the old man is there for keeps."

Lagana smiled, looking pleased.

Stone finished his drink and gave Larry the glass. "Fix me another, will you?" he said. Lagana's talk about his family made him irritable for some reason. The boss sounded like a damn queer, he thought. "Take off your coat," he said to him. "How about a drink?"

"No thanks, Max. I can only stay a minute. Some friends are coming over tonight, and I have to be home. Just people in the block, but I'm stuck as host."

God, are we respectable, Stone thought, taking his drink from Larry. "Well, let's get this wound up then," he said. "Debby, go downstairs and see there's plenty of food in. Some characters are coming in for poker." He nodded at her to get going. "Some hot corned beef would be a good idea."

"Okay, I'll tell Alex to send out for some," she said. She smiled and sauntered from the room.

Lagana put his hands in his suitcoat pockets and turned to Larry. "Well, you messed up that Bannion job nicely," he said, in a tone that matched his eyes. "Got it smeared all over the papers, and didn't get your man. Nice work, Larry."

Color came into Larry's face. "There won't be any more slip-ups," he said. "I thought the first arrangement was sure-fire. We cased it for a week, and Bannion put the car away every night. I—"

"It was stupidly handled from the start," Lagana said. "You should begin to use your head. A bomb in a car points right at us, gives the papers a perfect excuse to squawk. Hell, maybe you should get in the advertising business."

"Next time it will be nice and quiet," Larry said, trying to keep the anger from his voice.

"No, you're out of it," Lagana said. "Max, did you get a man?"

"Yeah, a guy from Chicago. He's flying in, gets here tonight. I understand he's good," Stone said, looking at his drink.

"What do you mean I'm out of it?" Larry said.

"Well, what do you think I mean?" Lagana said, glancing at him sharply. "You're out of it, that's all. You leave Bannion alone. Max has got an out-of-town man to handle it."

Larry glanced at Stone, feeling cheaply used. "You might've told me, Max," he said.

Stone laughed at Larry's sullen expression. He liked Larry, and knew he was smart and tough; but he was cocky and it wouldn't hurt to knock him down a peg. "Bannion is out of your class, I guess," he said. "We need an old-timer to handle him."

"He's just another stupid cop," Larry said.

"You've got things to learn," Lagana said. "Bannion's not stupid. He was on our neck fast enough on that job Big Burrows did." He glanced at Stone. "And that's another thing. That was a stupid job, too. I gave you these two things to handle because the boys in Central and Northeast have got real trouble. And you loused them both up. This isn't Nineteen Twenty. Tossing that babe out on the Pike was just another bit of unwelcome advertising." He turned to Larry. "You know what Bannion's been doing, I suppose? He's checking to find out who made that bomb."

Larry smiled slightly. "Sure I know about it," he said. "He's tramping all over the city, wearing out his big, flat feet. And it won't do him one damn bit of good."

"You're sure?"

"The guy who made it is dead. He was a lunger. I called him to tell him to get out of town when I heard what Bannion was doing, but the people he stayed with told me he was sick, was on the way to the hospital." Larry grinned. "So I crossed my fingers and called the hospital a couple of hours later. They told me he'd died."

"Well, that's one break," Lagana said. "I want you both to understand this; everything has to be quiet until elections. I don't want one damn thing in the papers. That Bannion deal is the only exception. Got that, Max?"

Stone nodded and sipped his drink.

Lagana buttoned his overcoat and glanced at his watch. "Well, I've got to get going," he said.

"By the way, there's something I wanted to talk to you about," Larry said.

"Yes?"

Larry told him about the seaman he'd met, and of the man's contacts in Italy, and that he had been able to bring in three pounds of heroin. "It's first rate stuff, all set to distribute," he said, unable to keep the excitement from his voice.

Lagana stared at him in silence, his eyes cold and expressionless. Then he said: "Okay, you buy it from him, Larry. With your money. Then you wrap it up with a brick and throw it in the river. Tomorrow! Got that?"

"But, hell—"

"Damn it, you seem to be getting dumber instead of smarter," Lagana cut in angrily. "There isn't going to be even one ounce of dope in this town. Get that through your thick head." He paced the floor, his thin face white with rage. "I don't like discussions, I don't like having to tell you things twice. I tell you once, and that's all. Do you understand?"

"Sure, sure, I understand," Larry said, swallowing hard.

Stone nodded and sipped his drink. This was more like it, like the old days. The boss was tough enough and smart enough to handle anything.

Lagana frowned slightly and looked from Larry to Stone. "Things are changing in this country," he said, in a quieter voice. "A man who doesn't see that hasn't got eyes. Kefauver didn't do us any good. But it's been building before that. The people are sick of us. We ran things the way we wanted to for a good long time. Dope, prostitution, gambling, political machines in our back pocket, we had the money, with strength to laugh at anyone in our way. But it's changed, I tell you. And if these coming elections go against our friends, we may not be able to make friends with the new crowd. With an honest ticket, which they've got, I'm sorry to say, we'll have Cranston to worry about the day after the elections."

"Cranston?" Larry shrugged. "The old snow-top in the Hall? What's special about him?"

"That old man is trouble," Lagana said. "Remember that. You'll stay out of jail longer if you do." He looked at Larry speculatively shaking his head. "You're not getting this, I see," he said. "Well, like they do with the kids in school, I'm going to tell you a little story. Try to get the point. Once upon a time," Lagana said dryly, "there was a guy in New York who ran the toughest union in the city. He was a friend of mine. This was in twenty-five. And then, being president of a big union in New York was like being the Democratic Candidate in Alabama. You were in. My friend Pete was a big man in local politics. His men made up the toughest union this country ever saw, and they breathed when Pete told 'em to. Pete was a king of the speaks. He had a manager and five waiters at his table, and nobody else in the joint got served until Pete was happy. He lapped it up like a thirsty cat."

Lagana put a cigarette in his mouth, and turned his head to find the match Gordon struck for him. "Thanks. Well, one night Pete had a big party and he saw a man across the room getting just as much attention as he was getting. This burned Pete up; he yelled for the manager to find out who he was. The manager told him it was Legs Diamond. You've heard the name?" Lagana said to Larry.

"Yeah, sure," Larry said, annoyed at the sarcasm. "So what happened?"

"Well, Pete stamped over to Diamond's table. 'They tell me you're Legs Diamond,' he said. Diamond looked up at him and said, 'So what if I am?' Well, Pete was a fancy dresser and he wore diamond clips on his garters. So he put a foot on Diamond's table, rolled up his trousers and then, being a jerk, said to Diamond, 'If you're such a rough one, try and shoot one of them clips off!' Diamond took a thirty-eight from under his arm and shot a hole through Pete's leg. Then he said, 'Get away from my table, lush, or I'll put the next one in your head.' " Lagana smiled. "That's all there was to it."

"Well, what happened next?" Larry said.

"Nothing happened, not one damn thing," Lagana said softly. "And that, if you've got the brains to see it, is the point of the story. Pete was carried out, and Legs Diamond went on with his dinner. Legs was a bigger man in New York than the boss of New York's biggest and toughest union. The cops heard about it, and looked the other way. That was the kind of weight we used to have; but it's gone, gone forever, Larry.

Now we try to look as respectable as possible, and keep out of the papers. Do you get what I'm telling you, Larry."

"I get the point," Larry said, casually.

"Okay, buy that dope from your friend, with your money, and throw it into the river. Got that? And don't ever touch that racket again in this town." He studied Larry, frowning slightly, his eyes as expressionless as cold little globes of glass. "You should be grateful the old days are gone," he said. "Then you wouldn't have got off with a little bed-time story about Legs Diamond. Keep that in mind. Come on, Gordon, we're late."

Lagana nodded to Stone and walked out the door.

When he was gone, when they heard the elevator whining in descent, Larry shrugged and made himself a drink. He glanced at Stone. "Well, what do you think of that?" he said.

"I think you'd better throw that dope in the river," Stone said, rubbing his bald head. Suddenly, he felt in excellent spirits. "Damn, I'm hungry," he said.

Ten

BANNION DROVE IN from Chester through a driving rain. He stopped inside the city line at a handbook and got Larry Smith's home address from the bookie. At the first drugstore he looked up his number, but got no answer.

That was fine.

He drove to the Parkway Building, a huge but elegant apartment house that featured uniformed doormen and a discreetly lavish atmosphere for anyone who could afford its prices. Bannion parked across the street from its gleaming, canopied entrance. He lit a cigarette and settled down to wait. His trenchcoat was wet, and drops of water were forming and falling from the brim of his hat. He put the hat on the seat without taking his eyes from the revolving door of Larry's building.

Larry would have to show eventually.

Bannion smoked and watched in the rainy darkness . . .

Larry left Stone's apartment at nine-thirty, bitter and disgusted. Max and Lagana thought they were big men because they'd been in the rackets in the twenties when (to hear them tell it) you got shot if you said boo to a mobster. It was all a lot of crap. They were kidding themselves, pounding their chests, treating him like a damn baby. Big men, real tough, he thought sneering. Bannion, a jerk of a cop, and Cranston, an old woman, had them shaking like a pair of nances.

Suddenly he rememberd the way Lagana had looked at him, up and down with those funny, blank eyes. Well, what the hell was a look? He put a tough smile on his face. Probably the old man needed glasses. Nobody had eyes like that unless he was dead. That's what the old man's eyes were like, he thought. Like a stiff's. There was a funny winter light in the back of them, the same thing you saw in a stiff's eyes.

Larry shivered slightly, and got into his car, ignoring the doorman's tip-twitching hand. What the hell was he thinking about the old man's eyes for? They were just eyes, like everyone had. Period. But he couldn't kid himself; he knew what was wrong when his thoughts skittered this way. He was afraid of dying, not the physical end of it, but what came afterwards. You went somewhere, up, down, out maybe, into space, and your body stayed behind, no use to anyone, cold and stiff. Larry had been raised a Catholic; he was afraid of dying because he'd left the church and knew he would be punished for it. But terrified as he was of this mysterious inevitable punishment, he was even more frightened by the conclusions of atheism. To go nowhere, to have it all end suddenly, forever, that was worse than anything else.

To hell with it, to hell with it, he thought, pounding the steering wheel with the heel of his hand. He pushed the ideas from his mind. Everything was going fine; tomorrow was wonderful, tomorrow was beautiful. He had been on his way home, but he changed his mind and drove to a flashy nightclub on Market Street. The hat check girl made a fuss over him, a couple of waiters hurrying through the velvet-walled foyer nodded to him and smiled, and Larry walked into the big dining and dancing room in a much better humor. This was a nice joint, a nice relaxing joint, he thought. Here they knew who he was, they knew he was a big shot.

Larry had been working for Max Stone for six years. He was number four man in Philadelphia, young for the responsibility, but that didn't prevent him from doing a good job. Larry was tough, smart, and completely without morals. He had come up through the ranks of a society that was founded on the fix; as a kid he'd delivered political handbills, driven voters to the polls, seen how the primary lists were padded with fictious names, and how the pressure was put on individuals who registered against the administration. Larry was no starveling from the slums. He had a high school education and his family were fairly decent, responsible people. Larry went into the rackets by choice, as another young man might go in for the law, because he had learned that everything was rigged —the police, the courts, politics, elections, the whole damn city. It was rigged like a slot machine to clip the suckers and pay off the operator. So why be a sucker?

He had his own handbook when he was twenty-one and then he went to work for Stone, in charge of a string of books on the West side. He arranged the pay-off, had quite a bit to say about applicants who wanted to open joints, and he handled the wire-service and all other details of the organization. Larry was a new element in the rackets, a type hand-picked by Mike Lagana. He was no Sicilian illiterate, no gun-happy hoodlum; Lagana wanted quiet young men, neighborhood boys, who were smart and tough but kept out of trouble. Larry didn't understand the higher strategy that had pushed him past a number of older men in the organization; he thought he was lucky, and he thanked the good old American way of things that rewarded industry and loyalty regardless of age, background or other irrelevant qualifications.

Larry ordered his dinner, oysters and a five-dollar steak, and settled back to enjoy the floor show. There was a girl in the line he hadn't seen before, a tall brunette with a good body and a wise, provocative expression on her face. He signaled the captain of waiters and pointed out the girl. "After the show ask her if she'd like to have a drink with me," he said, smiling.

The waiter smiled, too. "She'd like to, Mr. Smith."

It was funny how things changed. Half an hour he'd been in the dumps, but now he was riding high. Later, grinning over a drink at the brunette, he said, "Baby, you're just what I need. You saved my life tonight."

The brunette patted his hand.

Bannion walked up and down the sidewalk before Larry's building, a cigarette in the corner of his mouth. The rain had stopped and the early morning was cold and sharp. He glanced up at the big quiet apartment house, and rubbed a hand over his tired face. He wasn't conscious of fatigue; all he knew was the need to find Larry Smith, to get his hands on that loose end and jerk everything else into the light. But he'd have to wait; Larry had undoubtedly found some diversion. Well, enjoy yourself, Larry, Bannion thought. Enjoy tonight because you won't enjoy tomorrow.

Bannion had spent a bad five hours in the dark and rainy night, thinking of Kate. She had come back to him and he hugged the bitter loneliness she brought him because it was all he had left of her, all he had left in the world.

He flipped his cigarette into the street and walked over to his car, deciding to get something to drink before going back to the hotel. It had been some time since he'd eaten, but he wasn't hungry.

Most of the bars he passed were closed, so he drove on into the center of the city and stopped at one on Market Street. He settled down in a red-leather-covered booth in the rear of the place and asked the waitress to bring him a double rye.

There was a juke box sounding the currently popular songs, and a noisy table of college kids in the booth opposite him, good-natured boys having a big time drinking beer and kidding the waitress.

Bannion looked down at his big hands, trying to ignore the songs, the festive chatter from the adjacent booth. When the waitress brought his drink he told her to bring him the bottle. It would save her trips that way.

She said okay.

Twenty minutes later Max Stone came in, accompanied by Debby, and his bodyguard, a man named Jones. Debby took a stool at the bar and Stone shook hands with the manager. Jones took a seat at the end of the bar where he could watch the boss. Stone began rolling dice with a girl who sat behind a green-felt table. He lost consistently, and he wasn't happy about it. The money wasn't important, it was just a quarter a throw; but losing, on principle, made him sore. He had been losing steadily at poker in his apartment for the last four hours, and had taken a walk to let the run of the cards change. Stone felt like hell; he'd eaten four hot corned-beef sandwiches on Jewish rye bread and had drunk several highballs. They weren't doing him any good. He watched the dice bounce out of the leather cup he held, his eyes tired and narrowed. What was wrong with him? He'd felt better earlier in the evening, when Lagana had been putting it on the line to Larry. That was like old times. But when Mike had gone, Stone was swept with the familiar, anxious feeling that something was wrong, that everything was shifting under his feet.

"Don't pick 'em up so fast," he told the girl. "I want to look, too."

"Sure, Mr. Stone,"

The bartender smiled at Stone, the manager smiled at him, and Debby smiled at him; they knew he was in a touchy, explosive mood. Only Jones, his bodyguard, didn't smile; he wasn't paid to smile, he was paid to watch, so he sat at the end of the bar, a sullen-looking balding man, and watched Stone, watched the people who walked behind him, with gray, careful eyes.

"Don't pick 'em up so fast," Stone said again, glaring at the girl. "I'm not talking just to make noise, baby."

"No, of course not, Mr. Stone," the girl said, with a quick nervous smile.

A minute or so later, Stone swore violently. "You're cheating me, damn you," he yelled, and slammed the leather dice cup against the wall. He drew his thick arm back and slapped the girl across the face. The blow caught her by surprise and almost knocked her off the stool. She scrambled to the floor, and cowered in the corner, staring at Stone with wide, terrified eyes, too stunned to say anything.

The bartender began polishing a glass industriously, and a man at the bar who recognized Stone picked up his change and moved inconspicuously toward the door.

The manager put a hand nervously on Stone's arm. "Max, forget it, please," he said. "I'll pay her off tonight, chase her the hell out of here."

"What kind of a joint are you running?" Stone said, shaking the hand from his arm.

There was a buzz and stir as customers at the bar and in the booths turned to watch the disturbance.

Stone shoved his hands into the pockets of his overcoat and

stared down the room, watching one pair of eyes after another melt away from his angry, self-righteous glare. "Well, what're you looking at?" he snapped at a thin young man in a natty suit.

"Nothing, nothing at all," the young man said, and turned away with a weak smile.

The joint's bouncer, a stocky man in a dark blue suit, stood behind Stone, ready to move fast if anyone bothered him. Jones slid off his stool and was watching too, his weight balanced lightly, expectantly on the balls of his feet.

The only sound was the dice-girl's muffled sobs.

The college boys in the booth next to Bannion's had stood up for a better view of the excitement. One of them, a husky, clean-cut lad, looked uncertainly at his friends. "Hey, that big bastard slapped a girl," he said, with more surprise than outrage in his voice. He wet his lips, and then his face, his good humored, still unformed face, hardened. "Well, we'll see about that," he said, and his words sounded clearly in the silence.

He stepped from the booth and started toward Stone.

He didn't get very far. The man named Jones moved to meet him with a fast, springy stride. He bumped squarely into the boy, put both hands against his shoulders and shoved him powerfully back toward the booth.

"Where are you going, hero?" he said, coming after the boy, his hands swinging low at his sides.

Two waiters grabbed the boy's arms and shoved him down in the booth. He struggled against them, making only a token resistance; his face was white and scared. One of the waiters said, "Jeez, kid, don't be dumb. That's Max Stone. Get it, Max Stone. Keep your nose out of his business."

"He hit the girl," the boy said in a high, shaky voice.

"Okay, okay," the waiter said. "So he hit a girl. He can do what he wants." The waiter looked up at Jones, smiling nervously. "They're good kids, really. Just kind of excitable," he said.

Jones stared down at the college boy. "Don't be excitable, Junior," he said. "It don't figure."

Bannion raised his head slowly. Jones was standing just a few feet from him and his voice had fallen like an ugly weight across his thoughts. Keep out of it, he said to himself, and his lips moved with the silent words, almost as if he were praying. He had recognized Stone, the top man in West, and had heard the hassle. He knew Jones, too, a sullen punk who was happiest when crowding scared little people into a corner. Keep out of it, he said again, muttering the words aloud. He had his lead; Larry Smith. That might lead to Stone, but it had to be proved. There was no percentage in tipping his hand, making a move that could ruin his chances. He told himself to keep out of it, almost savagely, fighting the red anger that was sweeping through him, the anger that could destroy him along with everything in its way.

Jones' voice came down across his thoughts again, hard and contemptuous. "It don't figure, college boy," he said. "Don't be excitable. Remember that, Junior."

The glass shattered in Bannion's tightening fist. He stood and stepped into the aisle between the two rows of booths. "Hello, punk," he said to Jones.

Jones turned quickly, his lips drawing tight against his teeth. He looked up at Bannion and some of the bored, sullen toughness left his face. "This isn't any business of yours, Bannion," he said.

Bannion took the lapels of Jones' coat in one hand and pulled the man close to him. "You tell me what my business is, punk," he said, in a low, trembling voice. "You tell me all about it."

Jones wet his lips and tried to meet Bannion's eyes. "I—I got nothing to tell you, Bannion."

Bannion held the slack of Jones' coat in one big hand. He raised his arm slowly and lifted the man up to his toes. "You're a smart little punk," he said, in the same low voice. "Don't ever tell me anything." He turned Jones around and pushed him to the rear of the room. "Stay there and keep quiet," he said. "You're getting a break, remember."

Bannion looked at him for an instant, and then turned and walked toward Stone, moving slowly, deliberately, his hands jammed deep into the pockets of his trenchcoat. Under the rain-darkened brim of his hat his face was hard and expressionless.

"You like working girls over, don't you, Stone?" he said.

Stone glared at the big detective, seeing the brutal anger in
his face, and sensing the sudden, explosive quietness in the
room. He knew Debby was watching him; he couldn't let her
see him talked down, and he was in no mood to take anything
from anybody tonight. "Don't make a mistake, Bannion," he
said. "Don't play hero with me."

"You like working girls over, don't you?" Bannion said
again. He knew now what he was going to do; he would kill
Stone. He knew it was stupid, knew it would ruin everything,
but he was helpless in the grip of rage.

Debby watched the two men smiling, her chin cupped in the
palm of her hand, one gold sandaled foot swinging slowly. She
had never seen anyone treat Max this way before, and she
found it exciting and oddly satisfying.

The bouncer behind Stone looked at Bannion uncertainly,
remembered certain things he'd heard about him, and backed
slowly out of the picture.

Stone saw something in Bannion's face that cut off the
angry blustering words coming up in his throat. He knew Bannion was ready to kill him; this wasn't just mouth-work, this
was murder. Stone was suddenly cold and empty; it had happened so swiftly, so inevitably, he had no time to get ready for
it. It was like a bomb going off in your face. He laughed,
unaware that he was laughing, but heard the shrill sound of it
high above him in the air. His hands rose of their own voli-
tion, and his thick fingers fluttered up there in the curious,
strained noise of his laughter.

"Hell, Dave, take it easy," he said. "Take it easy. I'm
sorry, Dave, I'm sorry, I didn't know . . ." The words strung
out meaninglessly.

Bannion got himself under control. It was a struggle that
left him pale and shaken. "Get out of here, Stone," he said.
"Fast. While you're still alive."

Stone brought his hands down slowly. He glanced around
the room, quickly, uncertainly, seeing nothing, and then
turned and strode out the door. Bannion looked back at Jones
who stood motionless in the rear of the room. "You, too," he
said.

Jones walked quickly up to the bar, avoiding Bannion's
eyes, and hurried out after Stone. Bannion stood alone, rub-

bing his forehead, unaware of the sudden nervous laughter in the room, the excited burst of conversation, the renewed clink of glasses. He glanced down at the manager who was at his side. "I owe you for about half a bottle of rye," he said.

"No, no, forget it," the manager said, rubbing his hands together nervously.

"You'll be accused of buying me a drink."

The manager smiled tightly. "Always joking, eh?"

"You can relax, I'm leaving," Bannion said.

The manager came with him to the door and put a hand on his arm. "Dave, I'm proud to buy you a drink," he said, in a low hurried voice. "Believe that. You know I gotta take what comes in through the door, and—some of it stinks."

"Well, thanks," Bannion said, after a slight pause. "Tell you what; buy that college boy a drink, too. Tell him I said his heart's in the right place."

"Sure, Dave, sure."

Bannion walked down the block, his shoulders hunched against the wind. It was three-thirty in the morning. Market Street was empty except for a sailor wandering toward a subway entrance with his arm around a girl. Wind stirred refuse in the gutters, cigarette stubs, newspapers, numbers slips, and the bell of St. John's was tolling the milkman's mass.

He heard footsteps behind him, the fast clicking of high heels, and he stopped shortly and turned around. The girl was a smiling, happy-looking blonde, coming toward him with long, quick, graceful strides. She was pretty, the way dolls are pretty, and wore a mink over a black cocktail dress.

"Darn, you walk fast," she said.

"Well, not too fast, obviously," Bannion said. "What's on your mind?"

"I just thought I'd like to talk to you," Debby said. "I'm Debby Ward. I'm Max Stone's girl, by the way, although you wouldn't know it the way he left me back there like an overcoat or something he forgot."

"I know who you are," Bannion said.

"Well, fine, we know each other then," Debby said. "The bartender told me who you were. Your name is Bannion. A mick, aren't you?" She slipped her arm through Bannion's. "You want to walk along awhile?"

"I'm going home," Bannion said.

"Where's home?"

"A hotel room."

"Darn, I was hoping we could have a drink."

"What's your interest in me, Debby?"

She tilted her head. "I don't know. I liked the way you looked, that's all."

They walked along together in silence for a block, and Bannion said, "We could have that drink in my room. Okay?"

"Okay."

"You make up your mind in a hurry, don't you?"

"Uh huh," Debby said, and smiled . . .

Bannion made two drinks, rye with water, and handed one to Debby. She had made herself comfortable on the bed, pillow punched up behind her back, her slim, dancer's legs stretched out before her and crossed at the ankles. Bannion sat in a straight-backed chair and studied his drink.

"How is it being Max Stone's girl?" he said. "Fun."

"Sure. What have you got against him?"

"I just don't like him."

She laughed. "That's silly. You can't get anywhere in this town not liking Max."

"I'm not trying to get anywhere, Debby. Do you know Larry Smith?"

"Sure I know Larry. He was at Max's tonight. And Mike Lagana." She sipped her drink. "Business must be terrible. Mike never shows up unless something's wrong."

"Well, what's wrong?"

She shrugged. "Search me."

"That might be fun," Bannion said, and she laughed.

"What was on their collective minds?"

She smiled at him. "You're trying to pump me. That's okay, but honest to God I don't know a thing. What's more I don't want to know a thing. When the boys talk business I go out and get my legs waxed, or something."

"What did you come up here for, Debby?"

She looked at him and shrugged. "I guess I just wanted to needle Max. I don't like men leaving me in barrooms."

"You're going to teach him a lesson, eh?"

She colored slightly. "That isn't all of it, Bannion. I wasn't kidding when I said I liked the way you looked. At him, I meant. It's funny, but sometimes I feel just the way you looked tonight. He's a good guy, but—" She shrugged and smiled. "I'm not kicking. That's the way it is with every guy and gal, I suppose. You put up with the bad, take the good."

"And the good is pretty good?"

"I like it," Debby said. "Why shouldn't I?" She raised her eyebrows. "I've got all the clothes I want, I have a nice life, plenty of travel, nightclubs, excitement. What's wrong with that?"

"It's okay if you like the guy."

"He's all right."

"And if you don't care where the money comes from," Bannion said.

"Oh, stop it," Debby said, with a little laugh. She drew up her legs and locked her hands around her silken knees. "So Max is a gambler. Is that a crime? I know people who do lots worse and are in church every Sunday looking respectable as judges. And why should I care where he gets his money? The main thing is to have it. It isn't easy to get hold of, believe me. Nobody ever gave me anything until I met Max. I worked for what I got, I can tell you. I worked for my living. Living. That's putting it very fancy. Did you think I was some heiress before I met him, for God's sake?"

Bannion shrugged. "I didn't think about you at all."

"Well, there's a pretty speech for you," Debby said, sighing. "You're about as sentimental as a pair of handcuffs, I'll bet. Didn't you ever tell a girl nice things, Bannion? You know, hair like the west wind, eyes you could drown yourself in, skin like velvet. No?"

Bannion looked down at his drink. "Yes, I remember some things like that," he said slowly. He was silent a moment. Then he said, "Shall I call you a cab, Debby?"

"Well, I get the point," Debby said. She stood and smoothed the skirt of her dress, an embarrassed little smile on her lips. "Did I say something wrong, big boy?"

"No."

"Well, I like to know if I break the house rules."

"There aren't any rules here," Bannion said. He put his hand on her arm as they went to the door.

"What's the matter? Afraid to make a pass at Max Stone's girl?"

Bannion didn't answer.

Debby was trembling slightly. Something about this big, hard-faced man touched her in a curious way. She felt like squirming under the touch of his hand. "Do you really want me to go?" she said, turning at the door and coming close to him, so close that the points of her small, firm breasts touched the rough fabric of his jacket.

"You're Stone's girl," Bannion said, dropping his hand from her arm. He felt disgusted with himself, betrayed and shaken by his need. "I wouldn't touch anything of Stone's with a ten foot pole."

Debby colored and put a hand to her throat. "That's a rotten thing to say," she said.

"Goodnight Debby. Have a nice time. Buy another mink, get your legs waxed, roll in it."

"Bannion, what's the matter?" Suddenly, without reason, she wanted to be close to him, to have him like her, but she was afraid of him, afraid of the look in his face.

Bannion slammed the door on her and then stood with his back to it and stared bitterly down at the small, soft indentation her body had made in his bed.

Eleven

MAX STONE LET himself into his apartment and kicked the door shut behind him with savage anger. From the closed doors of the dining room came the noise of laughter and conversation. There was a man in the living room sitting on the sofa. He got to his feet as Stone entered. "You Max Stone?" he said.

Stone eyed him up and down. "Yeah. Who the hell are you?" He was eager for something, anything, to use as a target for his rage.

"My name is Hoffman, Joe Hoffman, from Chicago." Hoffman was a tall, loosely built man of forty or so, with thin, bony wrists and mild eyes. His hair was yellow and needed cutting. He looked like someone's country cousin on a first visit to the big city. "Sylvester Ryan said you needed a man," he said.

"Oh, yeah," Stone said. He shook hands with Hoffman, some of his anger ebbing away. "Yeah, I need a man. How the hell is Sylvester?"

"Just fine. He told me to give you his best," Hoffman said.

"Great guy, great guy," Stone said. He put his overcoat on a chair and lit a cigar, studying Hoffman appraisingly. "This guy is an ex-copper named Bannion," he said. "There can't be any slip-ups. Understand?"

Hoffman nodded. "Sure," he said.

"Bannion's a pretty sharp character," Stone said. "He was a cop, and he knows the score. He'll have a gun and can use it. You got to be careful."

"All right, I'll be careful," Hoffman said. "What else do I need to know?"

Stone described Bannion to Hoffman, told him what kind of car he drove, and where he was living. "I want this handled by tomorrow night, if possible," he said.

"Glad you said if possible. I do a job when the time is right and not before. What's a good hotel in this town?"

"You can stay here if you want."

"No, I like to be alone when I'm working. I can dope everything out better that way."

"Anything you say." Stone gave him the name of a hotel. "When you do the job get right back to Chicago. I don't want any connection with us on this one. I'll send your dough through Sylvester. That okay?"

"Perfectly okay. Sylvester said you were tops and that's good enough for me. By the way, he sent you a present," Hoffman said. He picked up a large, flat, carefully wrapped package from the sofa and handed it to Stone.

"Well, what d'ya know about this?" Stone said, smiling. He removed wrapping paper from a wooden box that was about two inches deep and a foot square. Stone raised the lid of the box and began to chuckle. Inside, surrounded by dry ice, was an unbaked pizza pie, covered with thinly sliced tomatoes and cheese, and crisscrossed with strips of anchovy.

Hoffman grinned at Stone. "It's from Antonio's Cellar, ready for the oven. Sylvester said you'd remember the place."

"Know it?" Stone laughed, staring delightedly at the pizza. "Sure I know it. Sylvester and I eat there every time I can get to Chicago. Hell, Antonio's got the best pizza in the world. Damn, this was a sweet thing for Sylvester to do. Imagine him remembering." He looked away from Hoffman, touched oddly by the gesture. "What a sweet guy," he said. "They don't make 'em like that anymore."

"Well, he thought you'd like it," Hoffman said, picking up his hat and briefcase from the sofa.

"You tell him I thought it was a damn fine thing for him to do," Stone said.

"Okay, I will, Max."

They walked to the door together and Stone patted Hoffman on the back. "You get some rest now. And remember, this job is important to us."

Hoffman nodded. "You can depend on me, Max."

When he'd gone Max strode into the dining room where the poker game was in progress. There were four men at the table, Judge McGraw of Quarter Sessions, a magistrate, and two professional gamblers from Jersey. Stone showed them the pizza, feeling warm and happy. This little gift, a silly sentimental thing for Sylvester to have done, had helped to erase his bitterness and anger. He gave the pizza to Alex and told him to put it in the ice box. "Get some Chianti tomorrow morning, and we'll have a real guinea lunch," he added. He sat down at the table, pulling his tie loose and grinning at the players. "Okay, let's have a little action now. You guys are in for a rough time."

"We shall see, we shall see," Judge McGraw said, smiling. He was a tall, handsome man with a theatrical head of white hair. In the courtroom he was famed for his great, echoing voice, and his stern, scholarly lectures on Godliness and morality.

"Okay, deal somebody," Stone said, cheerfully.

Half a hour later his mood had turned black once more. The cards ran against him, illogically, perversely. It was five card draw, no limit, open on anything. He couldn't buy a pot; he played close, he played recklessly, but nothing worked. He hardly glanced up when Debby came in, and sang out a hello to everybody. She drifted around behind him and put her hands lightly on his shoulders.

"Winning?" she said.

"No, and shut up," he told her.

"Well, you're in a sunny mood."

"Okay, okay, talk then," he said. He held an ace kicker to a pair of tens. McGraw threw away one card; two pair Stone thought gloomily. He picked up his cards and found another ten. Three tens. He bet recklessly, angrily, into McGraw's probable two pairs and got raised twice, heavily, for his trouble. "All right, all right," he said, calling. "What the hell are you so proud of."

Judge McGraw, chuckling, put down a flush.

Stone tore up his cards and threw them into the air. "Get a new deck, damn it." He glared at McGraw, feeling mean and unfriendly. "Filled a four-card flush, eh? You could come out of a latrine with violets in your hair. How do you do it?"

"It's just the smile of Lady Luck," Judge McGraw said. "Your turn will come, Max, my boy." He coughed and put a hand to his mouth, glancing quickly, casually at his watch. He hoped some excuse to break up the game would come along soon.

"Where the hell have you been?" Stone said to Debby, as Alex put a tray of coffee at his elbow.

"A fine time to be asking," Debby said. "You left me stranded, I noticed. Why should you care where I've been?"

Stone lit a cigar, his hands trembling. He felt a quick bitter stab of anger. He didn't like remembering that she had seen him hightail out of that bar like a scalded cat. Bannion would pay for that, by God. "I had to leave you there," he said, ignoring the questioning glances of the other players. "That guy is nuts. Come on, come on, somebody deal."

"He's not nuts," Debby said, enjoying his irritation. "And, in case this is news, he's pretty sore at you."

"Yeah? Who's been talking to you?" Stone didn't pick up his cards. He stared at his big, limp hands. "Who's been talking to you, I said."

"Why, Bannion, himself," Debby said, airily.

Stone stood so quickly that his chair over-turned with a crash. "You been talking with him?" he said.

"Sure, I've been talking to him," she said.

"Where did you see him?"

"I—I just bumped into him," Debby said. She knew she'd been foolish to needle him. "You're right, he's a nut, all right."

Stone was shaking with anger. He caught hold of her wrist and twisted it sharply, forcing her half-way to her knees. "Where'd you bump into him?" he yelled.

Debby cried out in pain. " Max, stop it!"

"Where'd you see him?"

"Let me go! Max, *please!*"

"You talk first."

"I just met him on the street," Debby said, her voice high and tight with pain. "Damn you, Max!" she said, starting to sob. "You walked out on me, didn't you?"

"Where did you go with him?"

"Max, you'll break my arm," Debby said, pushing futilely at him with her free hand.

Judge McGraw cleared his throat, his lean handsome face pale and anxious. "I suggest we all relax a bit," he said.

"I suggest you shut your mouth," Stone snapped.

"You're real tough with women," Debby said, crying. "But you weren't so tough with Bannion."

"Where'd you go with him?"

"I went to his hotel room, that's where."

Stone dropped her arm. He opened and closed his big hands, feeling the hate pumping sluggishly through his veins. "Damn you, damn you," he said, in a low, hoarse voice. She'd probably crawled into his bed, too, laughed with him about how old and weak Stone was becoming, and how he'd run out of the bar at the look in Bannion's face. "You bitch," he said, shouting the words into her pale, frightened face.

"Max, you act like you're out of your head," Debby said, still weeping. "You're the one who's nuts, not him."

"You bitch," Stone shouted again. He glared around wildly, and saw the steaming coffee pot on the table. Without thinking, without willing the action, his hand moved; he scooped it up and hurled the scalding coffee into her face.

Debby screamed and staggered backwards, clawing at her face with both hands. She collided with a chair and fell to the floor, her body jack-knifing spasmodically, and her gold-sandaled feet churning and kicking wildly. She stopped screaming almost immediately; the only sound that came from her was a ghastly choking noise, like that of a child who has sobbed itself to the point beyond exhaustion.

Judge McGraw was on his feet, rubbing his well-kept hands together in a gesture of entreaty. He glanced around, as if looking for some place to hide, and then said, "The girl is hurt, Stone. We—we must do something for her."

Stone rubbed his face. "I shouldn't have done it," he said, in a low, confused voice. He seemed unable to move or think;

he stared down at Debby's slim, twitching body and rubbed his face with a hand that had begun to shake.

One of the gamblers from Jersey, a big man with black hair, said, "Well, let's don't just stand here," and knelt beside her and shook her shoulder. He tried to pull her hands away from her face but she began to whimper like an animal in a trap. She lay doubled up on the floor, her knees drawn up to her chin, her gold-sandaled feet still at last. The coffee had soaked her dress and darkened her blonde hair in dirty, ugly patches.

Judge McGraw glanced at his wrist watch, and the magistrate, a small soft man with cautious eyes, started to get into his coat. They all watched Stone, except the man who was on the floor beside Debby.

Stone shook his shoulders, and the numb, glazed look cleared from his face. "Yeah, we got to take care of her," he said. He glanced at the magistrate. "Ben, you and Joey get her a doctor. Right now, fast."

"Hey, Max, this ain't my baby," the magistrate said. Joey, the gambler still at the table, swallowed hard, and said, "I got to beat it, Stone. Damn, I got—"

"Shut up," Stone said. "Get your coats on and get her to a doctor. He can fix her up."

"Where can I find a doctor now?" the magistrate said, rubbing his hands together nervously.

"You'd better find one," Stone said. "Maybe you can find the one who kept your son out of the army. Fast, I said. Damn it, move. I want her fixed up, understand."

The man moved quickly, guiltily, under the prod of his voice. The lifted Debby between them and carried her into the living room. Stone went ahead of them and picked up her mink from the chair she'd dropped it on. He wrapped it around her shoulders, and said, "Go on, go on! Get moving." Debby's hands were still locked over her face. Stone swallowed the fear in his throat, and said, "Let me know what the doc says. Stick right with her till you find out. Got that?"

"Sure, Max." They went out, both gamblers and the magistrate.

When the door closed behind them Stone walked heavily back to the dining room. Judge McGraw was getting into his overcoat.

"Where you going?" he said, pouring himself a drink.

"Well, the game seems to be over," Judge McGraw said smiling. "I thought I'd—"

"Sit down, sit down," Stone said. He shuddered slightly after finishing the drink. He didn't want to be alone. The room seemed to be echoing with Debby's screams. Why had he done that to her? "I said, sit down," he said. He poured himself another drink, a stronger one, and sat down with his big forearms on the table. "Come on, we can bump heads, judge. A little action is what we need."

"You know my weaknesses too well," the judge said, removing his overcoat.

"You know I didn't mean to do that," Stone said. "You know that, don't you? I'm not that kind of a bum. It's just that damn temper of mine."

"Sure, sure, Max," the judge said. He wet his lips. "I wouldn't worry about it too much." He couldn't afford a break with Stone. Not now. There was his boy in the Carmelites, and his three daughters, almost grown women now, looking up to him, comparing their friends to him, thinking of him as an ideal of honor and integrity. They had all enjoyed good schools, interesting vacations abroad, and the prospects of a secure future through his relationship with Stone. He couldn't risk breaking it off now. Not yet. Sometime, when they were all settled down, when they wouldn't be so badly hurt, then he'd break it off and risk the consequences. Sometime—the judge knew in his weak, worried, lonely heart that such a time would never come.

"Shall we make it stud?" he said pleasantly.

"Yeah, deal for God's sake," Stone said.

Twelve

LARRY SMITH PULLED up in front of the Parkway Building the next morning at ten o'clock. The day was bright and sunny, with a clean bracing wind blowing, and it suited Larry's mood perfectly. He had left the brunette from the nightclub several hours before, after a very gay night. She was good, all right, he thought, smiling as he left his car. That wise little look on her face wasn't misleading; she'd been around. He had stopped at a Turkish bath on the way home, a place where he kept a change of clothes, and had got the works; steam bath, rubdown, facial massage, shave. There was a ruddy color in his cheeks and his body was limber and relaxed, ready for a day of work, plans and excitement.

He was whistling as he opened the door of his modern, four room apartment, brilliant now with the morning sun. Everything was glinting with it; the bright yellow drapes, the blond, maplewood furniture; the cocktail shaker on top of the big combination bar and record-player. Larry was still whistling as he strode through the short hallway into the living room.

A hand struck his back and knocked him flying into the middle of the room.

Larry staggered forward, almost going to his knees under the force of the blow, and his gray, snap-brim hat bounded off his head and onto the floor. He turned quickly, confused and mad, his lips drawing back hard against his teeth.

A big man in a trenchcoat stood blocking the entrance to the hallway. His shoulders filled the opening, and his lined, tired face was as hard as a clenched fist.

"What the hell do you want?" Larry said.

"You know who I am?"

Larry moistened his lips. "Yeah. You're Bannion."

"Your first question was stupid then, Larry. You know what I want." Bannion came toward him slowly, his hands hidden in the pockets of his trenchcoat. "Let's don't make it messy," he said. "Let's just talk."

Larry faced Bannion, his legs spread, and forced a tough confidence into his face. "You're way out of line, friend," he said. "Don't make a fool of yourself. I'll have you locked up for breaking-and-entering."

"I haven't broken anything yet," Bannion said. "I used a pass key, a souvenir from my cop days. What job did Slim Lowry do for you?"

"You must be nuts," Larry said. He took a step toward Bannion, feeling suddenly strong and unafraid. This was the character Lagana and Stone were worried about, he thought. Another slob of a cop. "Look, turn your big tail and clear out of here," he said, snapping the words out harshly. "I got no time for dopes this morning. Go on, beat it."

Bannion's hands shot out, terrible hands on the ends of long, powerful arms, and closed relentlessly about Larry's throat. He pulled Larry close to him, slowly, effortlessly, ignoring the futile flurry of blows on his chest and shoulders. Larry's tongue came out between his teeth and his knees lost their strength. Only Bannion's hands held him upright.

"What did Lowry do for you?" Bannion said.

Larry tried to talk, but the words, loud and frantic in his exploding brain, died under Bannion's hands.

"You'll get one chance," Bannion said. "When I let go, start talking. If you don't, I'll finish the job." He opened his hands and Larry went down to his knees, gasping air into his cracking lungs, massaging his throat with his hands.

"Okay, talk," Bannion said.

Larry raised his head slowly. Bannion loomed above him, pitiless and terrible, a blurred, shimmering figure in his moist eyes. He had been close to the death he feared; his soul had been ready to slip away from him, to leave his body cold and hard and useless in the grip of Bannion's hands. He choked on the thought, and a vast, weakening self-pity welled up in him; he shouldn't be treated this way, he thought sniffling, he'd only been doing his job.

"They told me to get you," he said. The words came out in a high, relieved squeak. He caught Bannion's legs gratefully and pressed his face against the cold, smooth cloth of his trenchcoat.

"Who are 'they'?" Bannion said.

The voice was high above him, sounding from a place that was cold, lonely, remote.

"Stone, Max Stone. I got Slim to put the bomb in your car. We didn't want your wife." He shook his head, crying. "It was a mistake, you got to believe me."

"Why did Stone want me out of the way?"

"I don't know. Honest to God, I don't know."

He heard Bannion sigh; he tried to shout that he was telling the truth, but the hands were around his throat again, jerking him to his feet . . .

Bannion believed him at last. Larry lay huddled on the floor, shaking his head feebly, trying to touch Bannion's leg with one entreating hand. He couldn't talk; only his seeking hand expressed the love and fear of what had destroyed him forever.

"You're through, little man," Bannion said in a low voice. "I'm going to spread the word that you talked. Stone will know in an hour. Lagana five minutes later. You picked the wrong racket, little man. You might have been a happy book-keeper. Now you'll never have the chance."

He walked out of the apartment, closing the door softly, with a little click of finality, on Larry's sobs . . .

Bannion drove back to center-city through bright, winter sunlight. He stopped at a drugstore and made two telephone calls, both of them to men with wide contacts in the police and gambling sets of the city. He gave both the same story; he knew who was responsible for his wife's death. Max Stone. Larry Smith had talked. Neither of the men he called wanted to be involved; they were cautious, non-committal, relieved when Bannion rang off; but they were on the phone themselves a moment later with the news.

Bannion paused in the street to light a cigarette. A man approached him smiling awkwardly. "Can I borrow a light, mister?" he said.

"Sure."

The man was tall, with yellow hair that needed cutting, and thin bony wrists that stuck several inches out from the sleeves of his coat. He looked like someone's country cousin on a first visit to the big city.

"Nice day, ain't it?" the man said, still grinning.

Bannion held a light to his cigarette, and the man bobbed his head gratefully, and said, "Thanks, thanks a lot, mister."

"Don't mention it." Bannion flipped the match away and walked down the sidewalk to his car. The man with the yellow hair leaned against a building and watched him, smiling around the cigarette in his mouth.

Bannion drove back to the hotel, adding up the information he had gathered. It was the big boys, as he'd thought. Stone and Lagana, who had tried to get him, and had got Kate by mistake. He had been nosing about a No Trespassing sign, so they decided to put him out of the way. It had started with Deery's suicide. Lucy Carroway had thought there was something odd about it, and, for voicing her suspicions, had been tortured and killed. He had dug into her murder and had been taken off the case. Then, after he had tipped off Jerry Furnham of the *Express*, they had tried for him and got Kate.

Everything flowed inevitably from Deery's suicide. There must have been an angle to it he hadn't seen, something which spelled trouble for the big boys. They'd gone into action when Lucy Carroway had talked, closed the big fist. That was the way they preserved the *status quo,* kept their harmless, little city-wide bingo game operating. Kill, cheat, lie, destroy! While cops looked the other way and judges handed down suspended sentences. This was their city, their private, beautifully rigged slot machine, and to hell with the few million slobs who just happened to live in the place.

The desk clerk gave him his key, and said, "There's a woman waiting for you, Mr. Bannion. I sent her up to your room, because—well, there wasn't anything else to do. She was the one who was here the other night."

"I see, thanks. Are you sure she was alone?"

"Oh, yes, sir."

Bannion went up to his room and rapped lightly on the door. There was no answer, no sound from inside. He turned the knob gently, then pushed the door in and stepped aside. Nothing happened. The shades were drawn and an edge of sunlight cut into the darkness, spreading a suffused grayness over the worn rug. Bannion stepped into the room and saw Debby lying on the bed, her face turned toward the wall. He looked at her, annoyed and puzzled; because of the angle of her head he didn't see the bandages, immediately. When he saw them he frowned and closed the door.

"What happened, Debby?" he said, sitting on the edge of the bed.

She wasn't asleep; her eyes were open, reflecting the thin sunlight in tiny points. "I didn't have anywhere else to go," she said. "I couldn't—think of anywhere else."

"That's okay." He snapped on the bedside lamp. She turned her face from the light. "Don't do that," she said.

"Debby, tell me what happened."

She still wore the black cocktail dress, the gold sandals. There were ugly brown patches in her bright hair, and her face, the half of it that wasn't bandaged, was very pale.

"Max did it," she said. "After I came back last night. He threw coffee in my face." She began to cry weakly. "The big bastard. The big bastard. He doesn't care what he does to people."

"You've seen a doctor?"

"They took me to one, I guess. I woke up this morning in a room next to his office. I got up and walked out and came here. I—I couldn't think of anywhere else to go. Turn off the light, Bannion. Please."

"All right, Debby." He snapped off the light and picked up the phone. He told the operator, a cool and sensible woman, that he wanted another room on this floor for a friend of his, and a doctor.

"Can't I stay with you?" Debby said, when he put the phone down.

"Yes, I'm getting you a room."

"I want to stay with you. You're not afraid of him, are you, Bannion?"

"No, I'm not afraid of him," Bannion said. He took off his hat and coat and put them on a chair. She wanted sympathy now, protection, he thought, going into the bathroom for a glass of water. That was just dandy, except that he had no sympathy left for anyone.

The doctor got there ten minutes later, a plump balding man with a no-nonsene manner, and strangely kind, worried eyes. Bannion helped him get Debby into the adjoining room. They undressed her and put her into bed. The doctor gave her a sedative, and started changing the bandages on her face. She pushed at his hands, and said, "Don't look, Bannion. Please."

"Okay, okay," he said, and went back to his own room. He made himself a drink and raised the shade to let in some light. He sipped his drink, and stared out the window at a row of uniformly dull office buildings, and beyond them the switching tracks of the Reading. His thoughts turned slowly about Lagana, Max Stone, and finally, Derry. Thomas Francis Deery. The automatic little cog who handled the police department's paper work, who lived with a cool, detached blonde, and had had his fling with a blonde, a gay likable blonde, Lucy Carroway. What was so damn odd about that. Not much.

Deery had had a place in Atlantic City years ago; had he been taking a little cut then? Deciding, for some reason, to go straight, he had sold the place, and settled into an uneventful sort of life, enlivened only by his arm-chair traveling? Was that the way it had worked out? You desert the reality of Atlantic City and the pay-off for the unreality of Spain and the Fiji Islands. It was a nice, simple equation.

The doctor came in, looked Bannion up and down, and said, "I've got two prescriptions here to be filled. Who did that to her?"

"Her boy friend, which I'm not," Bannion said. "How is she?"

"Well, she's comfortable now," the doctor said, the coldness gone from his voice. "She should sleep."

"How about scars?"

"Probably. It's pretty hard to say." He put the prescription form on the bedside table. "See that she takes these according to the instructions. I'll be back tomorrow morning to take a look at her."

"Thanks, Doctor."

The doctor put on his overcoat and hesitated at the door. "Who's the boy friend, by the way? This is a police matter, if she'll prefer charges."

"I don't know," Bannion said.

"He shouldn't get away with this."

"Well, something may happen to him someday," Bannion said.

The doctor glanced at him curiously, and then cleared his throat and said, "Yes, yes of course. Well, I'll see you tomorrow."

Bannion went in to see her after the doctor had gone. The tension of pain had faded from her forhead, and her hands rested palely outside the covers.

"You're going to be oaky," he said. "You probably feel better already."

"That's the dope he gave me working," she said. "How'll I look, Bannion? Did he tell you?"

"He said you can't tell yet," he said.

"You talked to him about it, didn't you? Will I be scarred?"

"Settle down, Debby."

"Oh, sure, that's easy. What did he say?"

"There might be a scar. But that's not definite."

She was silent, her fingers playing restlessly on the covers. "A scar isn't so bad," she said. "Anyway, it's only on one side. I can go through life sideways." She turned her face to the wall. "He told you I'm messed up for good, didn't he?"

He lit a cigarette, and frowned slightly. She surprised him by saying, "You don't give a damn, I know. You're a real tough guy."

"It doesn't matter what I think," he said. He knew she was right; he was too cold and empty to care about anyone. He didn't care about her face, he wouldn't care if she solved her problem by jumping out the window. He wouldn't even be relieved; it simply made no difference.

"You can't live that way," she said. "Not caring about people, I mean. Not about me, but about someone. You ought to at least get a dog."

"Don't worry about me. Don't worry about anything, Debby. You'll be okay. Get some sleep now."

"I'll be okay when I get Stone," she said. "I'll get him, don't worry."

"Forget him, Debby."

"No, I won't forget him." Her voice was drowsy. "He'll wish I had, though, someday."

When she was alseep Bannion turned off the light and locked her door. He picked up his things from his own room, and the prescriptions, and went downstairs to the desk.

"This is important," he said to the desk clerk. "The girl in the room next to mine is sick. I want you to get these prescriptions filled for me, and don't let anyone go up to her room. Get that? I don't care if they claim to be her father, her mother, or her parish priest. Nobody sees her. If anyone tries to, you pick up the phone and yell for the cops. Use my name. Bannion. They'll know it, I think."

"Certainly. We'll be careful."

"Thanks very much."

Bannion left the desk and walked toward the revolving door. He was halfway there when a voice said, "Hey, Dave, wait a minute."

He stopped, turning, and saw Furnham, the *Express* reporter, and a tall, stooped, gray-haired man coming toward him; they had been sitting in a sofa at the side of the lobby. Their hats were still on a nearby chair.

"We were waiting for you, Dave," Furnham said. "This is my boss, Emmet Lehto, managing editor of the *Express*. He wanted to meet you."

Bannion shook hands with Lehto, who had a thin shy face and a pleasant smile. "Not only meet you, I want to talk to you," he said.

"I'm pretty busy now."

"Would you sit down long enough to have a cigarette?" Lehto said.

"All right."

They walked back to the sofa. Furnham collected the two hats and put them on a table. Bannion took the straight chair. "Well, what is it, Mr. Lehto?" he said.

"Have you been following the papers this week?" Lehto said.

"No, I haven't had time."

"Well, as editorial writers say, the administration has been under heavy fire," Lehto said, smiling slightly. "But it's probably not going to be enough to affect the elections. Something more dramatic is needed, I'm afraid. You know how people are. They see things, and still don't see them. They know about the politician-hoodlum tie-up in the city. They know that city contracts go to the hoodlum-controlled contracting companies, who cheat the tax-payer with sub-standard materials, and whose only thought is to squeeze as much profit as possible out of the job. They understand that ten or fifteen years of this causes the city's parks, schools, roads and public buildings to depreciate more than they would in fifty years of normal care and upkeep. Still they do nothing about it. Maybe they feel they can't; maybe they aren't angry. Our intention is to get them angry, Bannion."

"Well, that's fine," Bannion said, after a pause. "Let me wish you luck."

"We thought you could help us," Lehto said.

"I'm no newspaperman."

"We have more than news columns in the paper. There's an editorial page, too. If there's anything you want to say, any pressure you might like to exert, we could help you do it."

"I'm not interested in the sociological angles of corruption," Bannion said. "I'm after the men who killed my wife."

"We're after the same people. For that and other crimes. Do you see any reason why we can't work together?"

"Yes. You're crusaders. My motivations aren't so lofty."

"What difference does that make if we're trying to achieve the same result? Bannion, the people of this town need a firecracker under their tail. If we can slap them across the face with a big story, something they can't ignore, they may use their God-given but atrophying common sense and let some clear air into the city next month."

"A big story, eh? You think I've got one?"

"Yes, I do. Why was Lucy Carroway murdered? Why was your wife killed? Why does a cop have to quit the department to find answers to those questions? That's the story, Bannion."

"Possibly it is," Bannion said. "But I don't have it yet. And I won't get it here."

Lehto stood up, smiling rather reluctantly. "You want to work alone, I know. The trouble is the rest of us want to get into the act. It's a job that will be a pleasure to do."

"I'm hoping so," Bannion said. "Sorry I wasn't more help. Good bye."

There was a gray Chevrolet parked directly before the entrance of the hotel. Burke, from Homicide, was at the wheel, watching the revolving doors. When Bannion appeared, he climbed out of the car, his long face solemn. He pointed a finger at Bannion. "Bang!" he said softly. "Just like that, big boy." He wasn't smiling.

"Charades?" Bannion said.

"It ain't funny. Come here and meet our friend."

Bannion followed him to the side of the car. Carmody was in the back seat. He waved to Bannion. Shackled to his wrist, was a sullen-looking man with yellow hair that needed cutting.

"The hayseed is Joe Hoffman from Chicago, and he's no hayseed," Burke said. "You know him, Dave?"

Bannion stared at Hoffman, the long, awkward-looking man who might have been someone's country cousin on a first trip to the city. He remembered lighting a cigarette for Hoffman not two hours ago. "Yes! I've seen him," he said.

"Well, that's good," Burke said dryly. "You probably know that he's been tailing you around town all day. You probably also know that he works for Ryan in Chicago."

"No, that's news," Bannion said. He glanced at Burke. "I should say thanks, I guess. How'd you get him?"

"A cop at the airport recognized him when he got off the plane last night," Burke said. "This cop, who must be new on the job, passed the information on to the Hall. I mean, his sense of duty sounds like something only a new man would have."

"Yes, I got your fine sardonic touch," Bannion said. "Then what?"

"We checked the hotels and found him," Burke said. "Carmody and I started after him this morning, and he started after you. We picked him up about ten minutes ago. He was parked across the street in a rented car, with a forty-five on his knee." Burke glanced into the car at Hoffman. "I'm glad to say he's got no permit for the gun. We'll find out who brought him into town."

"I can tell you," Bannion said.

"The hell you will," Burke said, with a little smile. "I want to get it from him." He pointed a finger at Bannion. "Remember, big boy, it could happen. Stay awake."

"Okay," Bannion said.

Burke slapped his arm and got back into the car. It moved out from the curb, picked up speed and disappeared in the traffic.

"You may need our help, after all," Lehto said.

Bannion looked over his shoulder. Lehto and Furnham were standing just outside the revolving door of the hotel. Lehto's long, shy face was serious.

"You'll hear from me when I do," Bannion said.

He walked down the block, irritated and angry. This job was all his, his alone. He didn't want help from anyone.

Muscle had got him this far; now he had to use his head. The secret lay with Deery, a dead man. He would start with him now, the automatic little cog who handled the department's paper work and spent his nights reading about the bullfights in Spain, and the fertility charms of Pompeii.

Thirteen

MAX STONE HAD left orders with Alex not to be disturbed; he was in bed and he wanted to stay there, alone in the darkened room, until he felt able to get up and talk to people.

It was six in the evening and he'd been in bed all day, ever since Judge McGraw had left him at dawn. He hadn't been able to sleep; every time he'd doze off a splintered thought of Debby would pierce his mind, and he'd thrash about for a more comfortable position, hoping that the activity would banish the memory of her screams.

The door opened a crack. "Max, it's Lagana on the phone," Alex said. "I told him you weren't feeling well, but he said he has to talk to you."

"Okay, okay," Stone said.

Wearing nothing but shorts he padded into the small office he'd put in beside his bedroom. He picked up the phone. "Yeah, Mike, what is it?" He sat down feeling his heart pounding beneath his fat-armored ribs. "I've been in bed all day. What's up?"

"Wake up and stay awake," Lagana said in a tight, angry voice. "I've got enough to worry about in the Northeast without trouble from your area."

"What the hell's wrong?"

"The cops have that hot-shot you imported from Chicago,

131

for one thing," Lagana said. "Joe Hoffman. He was tailing Bannion and got himself arrested. What is he, a cub scout?"

Stone rubbed his aching forehead. "Ryan said he was all right," he muttered.

"That's a great help," Lagana said. "This is the second time you've messed up on Bannion. Now get this: leave him alone. Understand? Hoffman has admitted to the police he was here 'watching' Bannion. The *Express* already has a story on it. They want to know why Chicago hoods are imported to watch our former cops. There's been too much excitement in the city, and by God I want it stopped. Got it?"

"You think it's safe to let Bannion run around loose?"

Lagana said, in a cold, precise voice, "I want no more excitement. We'll take care of him after the elections. Maybe you can figure out some way to keep him harmlessly occupied until then, but no rough stuff. These papers are riding us and our friends, and it's got to stop."

"Sure, sure," Stone said.

"Okay. Now, another thing. You heard from Larry today?"

"No. I'm seeing him tonight."

"Maybe you won't. The word is around that he spilled to Bannion about who ordered that bomb put in his car. You heard nothing about this, eh?"

"No, I been in bed," Stone said.

"Well, get out of bed and stay out!" Lagana shouted.

Stone put the phone down and called for Alex. "What messages did I get today?"

"Magistrate Bension phoned. He said he took Debby to a doctor, but she walked out of the office this morning. He don't know where she is now."

Stone stood up glaring at Alex. "What the hell does he mean he doesn't know where she is?"

"That's all he said," Alex said. "He thought she might have come back here."

Stone pounded a fist into his palm. "I'll fix that bastard for this," he said. "All right, all right. Did Larry call?"

"No."

"Any other calls?"

"Not a thing, Max."

"Okay, fix me something to eat. Some soft-boiled eggs, I guess."

Still frowning, he picked up the phone and got in touch with Art Keene, his number two man. He listend to routine reports for a few minutes, occasionally saying, "Yeah, yeah," and then he told Art to get a couple of the boys, and come up to his apartment within the next hour. He hung up the phone and went in to shave and shower, trying to shake off this curious, leaden weight of anxiety and confusion. Debby was on his mind, and then this business about Joe Hoffman, and Larry. Damn that Bannion, he thought.

Art Keene and two other men arrived within an hour. Keene was a middle-aged man with thick, gray hair, and a lean, blank face. He never quite smiled, although he seemed often on the verge of it. The two men accompanying him were hand-book collectors; one was a nervous, affable man named Danielbaum, and the other was a big man with a wet-slack mouth and a head shaped like an artillery projectile. He was called Creamy.

Stone gave his orders fast. "I want you to get hold of Larry Smith," he told Keene. "Have him over here as soon as you can. You heard the talk, maybe?"

Keene nodded. "We'll pick him up, Max."

"Another thing." Stone glanced from one man to the other, rubbing his aching forehead irritably. "Debby's cleared out, and I want her back." He glared at them still massaging his forehead. "She can go to Siberia, understand, she's just an-other dame, but she's not walking off with the jewelry I bought her. That's all I want from her, understand."

Keene nodded, his face perfectly blank. "We'll find her, Max."

Stone began pacing the floor. "There's something else," he said, "Bannion. He's been bothering us. I don't want any rough stuff, but I want him kept busy. Too busy to worry about us." He glanced at Keene, then at the other two men. "Well, you got any ideas?"

"Bannion's child is staying with some of his relatives, I believe," Keene said.

"With his wife's sister," Stone said. "So what?"

"Supposing we try the routine they used to work on voters in the river wards. The ones who weren't voting smart, I mean. You know, a couple of magistrate's constables would bust in on them, carrying legal John Dow warrants, of course, and scare hell out of everyone in the house." Keene shrugged. "It works, Max. Most people are scared of warrants. The constables do a lot of loud talking, and maybe someone gets shoved on his fanny, accidentally, of course, and then they blow. It can be perfectly legal," Keene said, glancing at the backs of his hands. "Supposing we have a warrant issued charging Bannion's in-laws with disturbing the peace, loud parties, something like that."

"Who signs the complaint?" Stone said.

"That's immaterial. Somebody comes in and swears out the warrant, that's all. Later, if it seems that the complainant is non-existent, that's not the Magistrate's fault. Practical jokes happen, in the best-run wards."

"It would have to be done when Bannion wasn't there," Stone said.

"Naturally. I'll set it up, Max. Creamy and Danielbaum here can serve the warrants. They're both constables. You know the routine, don't you, boys?"

Creamy made a circle with his thumb and forefinger, and grinned.

"Say, they got a police guard at the home," Stone said, glancing at Keene. "Better take care of that."

"I'll give the captain a ring. No sense wasting taxpayers' money like that," Keene said, and this time he used one of his rare smiles.

"Okay, I want no slip-ups on any of this," Stone said. "That gag should keep Bannion close to home. He'll stick there watching his brat if he's human. And don't forget I want to see Larry Smith and Debby. That's important, too."

When the three men had gone Stone paced the floor chewing on an unlighted cigar. He needed something to break his restless, anxious mood. But nothing appealed to him; he was sick of gambling, of eating and drinking. Only Debby could help him, it seemed. He'd fix her when she came crawling back, he thought, pacing restlessly. He was suddenly glad, viciously glad, that he had hurt her, that he made her scream. She had it coming, and she needed more of it. He had a breathless, dizzying vision of beating her and laughing at her screams. She'd run out on him, hadn't she? After a moment or so, he glanced casually, guiltily over his shoulder. He felt oddly disturbed and vulnerable. Stone was sick and weak with a new knowledge of himself; and he knew then that he would never lay a finger on Debby again as long as he lived.

Bannion spent that day checking into Tom Deery. He began at the Hall, and looked up the title on his place in Atlantic City. It had been a six-room bungalow on the water, and Deery had bought it in 1939 for eleven thousand dollars. A heavy lump of money for a police clerk. Bannion drove out to Deery's block and learned from a talkative neighbor that Mrs. Deery had once been a great traveler, that she took frequent vacation jaunts to Miami, Palm Springs, places like that. Not anymore though, his informant, a grayhaired Irish-woman, told him with considerable relish. For the past eight or ten years Mrs. Deery had come down a peg or two in the world, and spent her time at home like she should have done in the first place.

Bannion digested this, thanked the woman, and drove back downtown. The Deerys had travelled high, and then low. Thomas Francis Deery had once known where to pick up extra change—that was obvious.

He left the car before the hotel and went up to his room. The phone began ringing, as he opened the door.

It was Parnell, the county detective he had met on Lucy Carroway's murder.

"I called Central Homicide to get in touch with you," Parnell said. "Man name of Burke gave me your hotel number."

"What's on your mind?"

"I'd like to talk to you if you've got the time," Parnell said.

"I'll be out in about an hour."

"Thanks, Bannion."

Bannion found Parnell in his office, a sunny, comfortable room, with a rug on the floor and photographs of the surrounding countryside on the wall. He shook hands with Bannion, smiling. "Good of you to come out," he said. "Here, sit down."

"Thanks."

Parnell sat down behind his desk, looking a bit like a country lawyer who hunted and fished, when work was slack. Bannion knew he was sharp, and that's why he'd dropped everything to come out and see him; Parnell had a deceptive general-store manner about him, and, under that, Bannion guessed, a clear, alert mind.

"I've been on Lucy Carroway's murder pretty steady," Parnell said. "I've turned up a lead, I think. One of our people out here, a doctor in Philadelphia, was coming home late after delivering a baby. He tells me he saw a blue convertible on the Pike about two in the morning, parked right about where I found Lucy Carroway's body. There was a man standing beside the car, the doctor says, a big man in a camel's hair coat. The doc wouldn't be able to pick that man out of a line, even though he did get a quick look at his face. He says the man was dark-skinned and with a prominent nose. It's really not such a hot lead, you can see."

"Well, what did you want to talk to me about then?"

"I knew you were working on the case in Central, and I remembered that you said this girl had been connected with Tom Deery's suicide. So I called Central City Homicide to find out if you'd come across anything that would tie in with my big-nosed stranger." Parnell paused a few seconds, regarding Bannion with an odd little smile. "I talked to a Lieutenant Wilks," he said.

"And what did he have to say?"

"He said you hadn't turned up anything on the girl's murder, and that your attempt to connect her with the Deery suicide was just a pipe dream. I don't think you're a pipe dreamer, or any other kind of dreamer, Bannion. That's why I wanted to talk to you."

"You're on a good lead," Bannion said. "Lucy Carroway left her hotel with a man who wore a camel's hair coat, was dark-skinned and had a big nose. That character's name is Big Burrows, a Detroit hoodlum, who had been working for Max Stone. He's left town since Lucy's murder—and she was murdered, remember, shortly after telling me there might be something queer about Tom Deery's suicide.''

"Funny he didn't tell me about this," Parnell said.

"I think my report has been mislaid by now."

"What's wrong with him?"

"They call it human nature," Bannion said.

"Well, it's human nature to feel as I do then," Parnell said rather grimly. "I'm going to keep plugging away at this one. I don't like Central City hoodlums using the Thruway as an execution block, and I don't like the idea of women being tortured and murdered."

That was the end of their talk. Parnell put on his coat and walked Bannion to his car. The air was cold and the darkness was pushing up from the ground toward the gloomy, purple sky.

"How about having a bite with me?" Parnell said. "Not at my home, because I know you don't want to meet a lot of strangers. But there's a lodge down the Thruway where they've got charcoal-broiled steaks, and honest drinks. What do you say?"

"I'm afraid not," Bannion said. "I——"

Parnell put a hand on his arm. "You've got to eat, boy. You've been driving yourself, haven't you?"

Bannion hesitated, then glanced at his watch. "Okay, let's have a steak," he said.

After dinner Parnell ordered extra coffee and brandy. There was a fire in the main room of the beam-ceilinged lodge, and the warmth of it, and the food and drink, worked some of the tension from Bannion's body.

"I haven't said anything about your wife," Parnell said.

"I appreciate that."

"Well, let me say this much; I hope you get the sons."

"I think I will," Bannion said.

"Is there any way I could help?"

Bannion shook his head slowly. He glanced at his watch. "Can I make a phone call from here?"

"Sure, there's a phone in the next room."

Bannion walked into the adjoining room and put in a toll call to Central City. He hadn't called Marg today, hadn't said hello to Brigid. It wasn't fair to saddle them with a worried, anxious child . . . The operator sang out, "Thirty-five cents, please," and he dropped in the coins, listening to them clatter ringingly into the box.

Marg's husband, Al, answered the phone. His voice was high and sharp. "Yes? Who's this?"

"It's Dave," Bannion said. "How's everything?"

"I'm glad you called. They've taken the police detail off the house. Marg—well, she's kind of worried."

"When did this happen?"

"There was no replacement after the cop left at six tonight. Marg called the station house, and they told her it was orders. They don't have the men to spare."

Bannion swore. He was an hour-and-a-half from their place, perhaps two in the night-time traffic. "There's nothing to worry about," he said. "This isn't Russia." Bannion knew they were just empty words. He knew trouble could come, to Al, Marg and Brigid. This was a way to hit at him through a four-year-old child.

"Everything's okay on this end," Al said. "I've——"

Bannion hung up on him and went back to his table. Parnell had already taken the check. "I've got to get back to town," Bannion said. "Can you give me an escort as far as City Line?"

"You're damn right I can," Parnell said, rising quickly. "Something wrong, eh?"

"Maybe."

"You follow me. I've got a fast car and a loud siren."

"I'll follow you," Bannion said.

Fourteen

BANNION WAS ON his own as he crossed City Line into Philadelphia. He slowed down to forty with the traffic and tried to keep his imagination and temper in check. They wouldn't try anything so raw, he kept telling himself; but the knowledge of what they'd done to Lucy Carroway, to Kate, mocked this self-delusion. Why should they stop now? This was their town and they did what they liked with it, and the people in it, whether they happened to be men, women or four-year-old kids.

The traffic thickened as he neared the center of the city. Finally he was through the worst of it, across the river and onto an artery that led out to Marg and Al's home. He opened up then, hammering the horn with a clenched fist, forcing the traffic to give way, slipping through changing lights inches ahead of right-angling cars.

They lived on Filmore Street, a tree-lined avenue of two-story apartment buildings. It was a dark, cloudy night; the street lamps' yellow cones barely reached as far as the sidewalks.

There were no lights in the living room of their apartment, Bannion saw, as he went up the stone walk to the entrance. Maybe Al was playing possum. Maybe anything.

He entered the dark vestibule and reached out for the bell of Al's apartment. Something hard jammed into his back, and a soft but business-like voice said, "Easy Mac! Get your arms away from your body and fast."

Bannion obeyed slowly, cursing his own carelessness.

"Okay, upstairs," the soft voice said. "Move nice and easy, big man." An arm passed around Bannion, the inner door was pulled open. "Up you go."

Bannion went up the stairs to the first landing. The door opened and Al looked out, a worried frown on his high forehead. "Damn, I'm glad to see you——"

"Shut the door!" Bannion snapped.

"Hold it, *relax!*"

Bannion spun sideways, slapping downward at the gun in his back. He struck the man's wrist instead, and heard a yelp of pain. The gun struck the carpeted floor and bounced down the steps.

Al grabbed his arm. "It's all right, Dave!" he shouted.

The man behind Bannion scuttled down the steps after his gun.

"What's going on?" Bannion said.

The man picked up the gun and looked up at Bannion with a crestfallen smile. He was slimly built, twenty-eight or thirty, with pleasant, intelligent features. "You're pretty fast, Mr. Bannion," he said. "I'm sorry about jumping you, but Al said to stop everybody, and I was just following orders."

"It's okay, it's okay," Al said. "Get back into the vestibule, Mark."

Bannion looked from the man with the gun to Al. "What kind of a stunt is this?" he said.

"Come in, come in and I'll tell you," Al said.

Bannion shrugged and walked into Al's apartment. "Well, what is it?" he said.

"He's a friend of mine," Al said, closing the door. "After I talked with you I got in touch with some of the guys I soldiered with in the Pacific. They're good guys. They came on the double."

Bannion was silent a moment. "They're taking a chance," he said.

"They know what they're doing. Look, Marg's in the bedroom with the kids. Come on in and meet the boys."

Bannion put his hat and coat on a chair and walked quietly

down the hall after Al. Three men were at the table in the dining room, their coats on the backs of the chairs. They were playing cards. It looked like a mild, friendly game. There were a half dozen bottles of beer on the table.

Al introduced them with a word or two of description; Bannion shook hands with Tom Bell, a stocky towhead who ran a garage; with a red-haired lawyer named Corcoran, and with Tony Myers, an insurance man who greeted him as warmly as if he were a prospective client.

Al poured a beer for him, and Bannion sat down slowly. He felt tired and slightly confused. The beer tasted good; it cleaned the dry taste of fear from his throat. He looked at the three men and shook his head. "You're all nuts," he said.

"Dave got past Mark," Al said.

They regarded him with new respect. "That boy's slipping," Tom Bell said. "You know, Mr. Bannion, Mark got himself a DSC on Okinawa, and out there that wasn't a theater ribbon. But he just can't take this civilian life, I guess."

Myers stood up, and said, "I'll go down and keep him company."

"Wait a minute," Bannion said. "You men mean well, but I can't let you do it. If trouble comes it will be from hoodlums who know their business, and won't be stopped by amateurs whose hearts happen to be in the right place. It's my job, boys."

Bell, the towhead, looked annoyed. "They're real tough characters, eh?" he said. "Just like you see in comic books, with guns and everything. Well, we ain't exactly the cast from a maypole dance, Bannion." He hitched around in his chair, and tossed his cards onto the table. "Look, I been places those creeps wouldn't go unless they were in a fifty-ton tank. And I went in on foot with nothing in me hand but a BAR. I——"

Corcoran regarded him with a pained expression. "Tommy, if this is the story of your single-handed occupation of the Philippines, remember most of us have heard it quite a few times."

"All right, big wit," Bell said, irritably. "I used to think it was for the birds. But in the back of my head I knew it had to be done. Keep our homes safe, all that soap-box stuff. Now you tell me some rough characters are going to walk in and knock off a four-year-old kid, and that I'm too soft to stand up to 'em. Well, I'll tell you something. Anybody comes in tonight with that idea is going to wind up dead, I tell you——''

Corcoran slapped him on the shoulder. "Ah, the patriot and poet is coming out now, eh my boy?"

"Ah, shove it," Bell said with an uncomfortable grin.

Corcoran glanced at Bannion. "Seriously, Bell is right. Unfortunately he's a Swede and lacks our fine Celtic sense of restraint and understatement. But he's putting it accurately, if with considerable personal glorification. Your little girl is safe. Myers and Mark are in the vestibule, and out in the back yard is a character we used to call the Chief. The Chief is an Indian, and a damned unnerving thing to meet in the dark. Inside there's Tommy, myself, and your balding brother-in-law, who distinguished himself as the only American soldier to go AWOL in a jungle consisting solely of coconuts, spiders and Nips." Corcoran nodded slowly, and now his face was grimly serious. "Everything will be okay, Mr. Bannion. You can count on that."

Bannion looked around at them all, and realized with a touch of wonder that these run-of-the-mill, law-abiding citizens had something that was probably more than a match for Stone, Lagana and their hard, brutal organizations. It was the power of simple, down-to-earth goodness.

"Well, you want to sit in, Mr. Bannion?" Tom Bell said, picking up the cards.

"No, thanks, I've got to go back downtown."

"Well, things here are under control. Remember that."

Al came with Bannion to the front door. "Don't take too many chances, Dave."

"I'm being careful. The break is coming. Look, tell Brigid I'll be out tomorrow. Tell her, well, tell her I'll bring her a surprise."

"All right, I'll tell her, Dave."

Bannion went quietly down to the vestibule. As he opened the door he heard Myers saying, in an insistent, crowding voice, "Now, Mark, the thing about a twenty-year endowment is this. You get——" He stopped and said, "You leave things in our hands, Mr. Bannion. We got this end taped."

"Thanks. Thanks very much."

Bannion stepped into the cold darkness, and checked the street right and left before starting down to the sidewalk. There was a man standing across the street, he saw then, a tall old man with a square, weather-roughened face. The man was under a street lamp and the light gleamed on his gold-braided shoulders, on the brass buttons of his blue overcoat.

Bannion paused, hands in his pockets and then strolled slowly across the street.

"Hello, Inspector," he said.

Inspector Cranston nodded smiling. "Hello, Dave."

"What are you doing here?"

"Just smoking a cigar. Habit of mine after dinner."

"Oh, sure. And always outside under a street lamp."

"I smoke it anywhere I please," Inspector Cranston said. "Tonight I'm smoking it here." He glanced at his cigar. "Might take some time to finish this one, too."

"You heard the police detail was pulled off here, eh?"

"Yes, that news got up to the Hall," Inspector Cranston said.

"And that's why you're here."

"I'm just smoking a cigar, I told you."

"Under the street lamp, and in uniform," Bannion said. He shook his head slowly. "You're a little old for a beat job, Inspector."

Cranston smiled slightly, a hunter's smile. "This was too raw to overlook, Dave. They might can a cop for butting into it, but not an Inspector. Go on with your work. Nothing's going to happen here tonight. That's a promise from—" he paused, and said bitterly, "from the Bureau of Police, Dave."

Bannion paused, oddly touched by this stern, honest, sad old cop. "I believe that," he said, at last. "Enjoy your smoke, Inspector."

"Goodnight, Dave, I will."

Bannion walked down the street to his car. There was another one parked behind his, and he saw the figure of a man sitting behind the wheel. He slid his hand under his coat to the butt of his gun and stopped. The man in the car cranked down the window, put his head out and called, "Hello, Dave." Bannion saw the light glint on his reversed collar.

Bannion let out his breath then and walked along to the car.
"Out on a sick call, Father?" he said.

Father Masterson had no flair for irony. "No, it's nothing
like that," he said, in a worried voice. "Al called me an hour
ago and said the police had taken their men away from the
house. He was upset about it—"

"What the devil did he call you for?" Bannion said.

"I don't quite know," Father Masterson said. "It's preposterous to think I could help, of course."

"I didn't mean that," Bannion said irritably. "But Al
shouldn't be alerting the whole city."

"Why not?"

Bannion had no answer to that, so he said, "Father, Al's
got friends of his inside, and Inspector Cranston is standing
out in the open across the street. An armored division couldn't
crash into that apartment tonight. Why don't you go back to
the rectory and have a cup of tea?"

"Well, that's a comfortable idea, but I think I'll stick it
out," Father Masterson said. "You know, Dave, it's a curious
thing but priests don't often get shot. Some may regard that as
a great pity, but it doesn't happen very frequently. A man will
shoot policemen, unarmed bystanders, women and children,
but something stops him from firing on a man who wears his
collar backwards. That's superstition, of course, a Medieval
hangover, you might say, but that's how it works. So if there's
trouble I might come in handy. By the way, there's a radical
element who might claim that the symbol of God, even a poor
symbol like me, has a discouraging effect on evil. But we're
way off the point, aren't we?"

"Okay, Father," Bannion said. "I've sounded extremely
stupid, I realize. I'm sorry. Good hunting."

"Why, thanks!" Father Masterson said with a pleased
smile.

Bannion walked to his car and slid in behind the wheel, feeling something other than hate inside him for the first time
since Kate had been murdered. Ahead of him the street looked
quiet and innocent. Living room lights shone comfortably into
the darkness. It was about as quiet and innocent as a ticking
bomb, Bannion thought, as he stepped on the starter . . .

Debby was awake when he returned to the hotel. She was in

bed and the lights were out, but she said, "Bannion?" in a quick scared voice when he opened the door.

"Yes, it's Bannion," he said. "How are you feeling?"

"Oh, I'm great," she said in a low voice.

"Mind a little light?"

"No, I guess not. I've got to get used to being looked at sometime."

Bannion turned on the bed-side lamp. He saw that she had put on lipstick, and had made an attempt to comb her hair. "You're looking better already," he said. She lay with her arms outside the covers, pressed close to her slim body, and her face turned toward the wall. "Oh, I'm a knockout," she said.

He got a glass of water from the bathroom and put her pills on the table. "It's time for these," he said. "Excuse me, I'm going to get a drink from my room." He didn't wish to embarrass her with his presence while she went about the clumsy business of sitting up and taking the pills. When he returned she was lying flat, her face averted; but the water and pills were gone.

Bannion sat down. "How about food? You must be hungry."

"I'm okay."

"You've got to eat. How about some chicken soup?"

"All right," she said. "I'm a damn nuisance, I know. Why don't you bounce me out of here?"

"Do you want to go?"

"—No."

"Okay, stop talking that way then," Bannion said. "I'll order something for you on my way out." He sipped his drink, frowning slightly, and then picked up her room phone.

"Are you going right out?"

"Yes, I must."

She smiled weakly. "Can't you talk to me for a little while first?"

Bannion hesitated and then put the receiver back in place. "This isn't much fun for you, is it?"

"Not much," she said. "I feel like something that's been shut up because no one wants to look at it. I just lie here and think, that's all." She smiled, but it was a lopsided effort.

"For a gal who spent most of her life not thinking, it's a pretty rough routine."

"It won't last forever."

"What was your wife like, Bannion," she said slowly. "I know she's dead. I remember reading about it. That's why you pushed me out that first night. Maybe that was the reason, anyway."

Bannion stared at her, his face perfectly still. "She was a tall girl, twenty-seven years old, with red hair and light blue eyes. She wore a size twelve dress, I think." He stopped and looked at the drink in his hand.

"That's a police description," Debby said, with a little laugh. "That doesn't tell me anything. Did she like to cook, did she like to be surprised, what kind of things struck her as funny—that's what I mean."

Bannion stood and walked slowly to the window. He stared down at the neon jungle of Arch Street, saw the rain shining on the car tracks, and two sailors running along the sidewalk, the collars of their peajackets turned up about their necks.

"I'm sorry, Bannion," she said in a low voice. "I'm a dummy. You don't want to talk about her. Not with me, I mean."

"I don't want to talk about her with anyone," Bannion said, coming back to his chair.

"I'm sorry."

"There's nothing to be sorry about," he said. He picked up the phone and gave the operator a number. He tried to push the tangled memories of Kate from his mind, for now, for just a little longer. This call might be the pay-off, the beginning of the pay-off.

"You going out?" Debby said.

"Yes, I'm sorry." The phone buzzed at the other end.

"There's nothing to be sorry about," she said, using his phrase deliberately. Her voice wasn't bitter, although she meant it to be; it was only unhappy.

The connection was made. A sharp, alert voice said, "Hello?"

Bannion motioned Debby to be silent. "Lieutenant Wilks?" he said.

"That's right. Who's this?"

"This is Dave Bannion, Lieutenant."

Wilks said hello again, quickly and heartily. They exchanged how-are-yous? and fine-thanks, and then there came a pause, a waiting humming silence. Bannion grinned without humor, and said, "The reason I called, Lieutenant, is that I'd like to see you tonight if that's possible."

Debby glanced curiously at Bannion. His voice was faintly tinged with entreaty.

"Well, let's see," Wilks said. "Actually, Dave, tomorrow would be better. How about dropping in at the office?"

"I'd rather make it tonight," Bannion said. "This is important, to me at least. I talked with Parnell, the county detective, this evening about the Lucy Carroway murder."

He waited, still smiling tightly, as the silence came again, the straining anxious silence.

"What's your interest in that murder, Dave?" Wilks said, at last.

"That's what I'd like to see you about."

"All right, come on out. I'll be expecting you," Wilks said. There was no pause this time; his voice was sharp and cold.

"In half an hour," Bannion said. He put the phone in its cradle and got to his feet.

"Gosh, butter wouldn't melt in your mouth," Debby said.

"It wasn't altogether an act. If I sounded worried, it's because I am," Bannion said. "Well, I'll have something sent up for you. I'll leave the key with you. Be sure to lock yourself in."

"You sound excited. Have you got a lead?"

Bannion glanced at her, understanding, and touched by her interest. She wanted to mean something to someone, to be a part, if only a verbal part, of some other human being's plans, hopes and needs. He felt for her a little of the pity that his hatred had denied to himself.

"Well, it's a try for a lead," he said. "Wish me luck, Debby."

"I do, I do," she said, in a low voice. "I hope you get them, Bannion. I hope you get them all."

"Thanks, Debby." He patted her hand and left the room.

Fifteen

BANNION ASKED THE desk clerk to have some chicken soup, crackers and tea sent up to Debby. The clerk said, "Right away, certainly." He paused, glanced around the lobby, then leaned closer to Bannion. "There was a man in asking about her five or ten minutes ago. I told him she couldn't see anyone, doctor's orders, and he said thanks and walked out."

"I see. What did he look like?"

"He was middle-aged and rather flashily dressed. I didn't like his looks, frankly."

Some character of Stone's, Bannion thought. "Okay, nobody sees her, remember that," he said to the clerk.

"Yes, sir, Mr. Bannion."

He wondered if he should call Debby, and decided against worrying her; she was okay for the moment. Stone could watch and wait now, until she tried to leave town. Then, if he still wanted her back, he could do something about it.

Bannion went out to his car and drove to Wilks' home, which was an unpretentious, two-storied house in the Northeast area of the city. The house was comfortably shabby, and blended nicely with its middle-class neighborhood. Wilks' establishment in Maryland was considerably more elegant.

Wilks answered the door and greeted Bannion warmly.

"Come in, come in," he said. "Nasty night, isn't it? I was

about ready to hit the hay when you called." He took Bannion's coat and hung it on an old-fashioned clothes tree in the hall. "How about a cup of coffee?" he said, ushering him into the warm, well-used living room.

"No thanks," Bannion said. "I know it's late, and I'll be as quick as possible."

Wilks laughed. "I'm always ready to sit up and talk. Here, take this chair, it's about the only one that you'll find comfortable."

Wilks sat down facing Bannion and re-lit his pipe. There was an evening paper on the floor at his feet, and the radio, which was within reach of his hand, was playing soft music. "Nice night to be inside," he said, when his pipe was drawing smoothly. "Now, what's on your mind, Dave?"

"I talked with Parnell this evening," Bannion said. "You know he's working on Lucy Carroway's murder."

"Yes, of course." Wilks looked interested, nothing more.

"He's come across a lead, a rather slim one, but it bears out my theory about that job."

Wilks took his pipe from his mouth. He said, "I don't see how this concerns me, Dave."

"Perhaps I can show you," Bannion said. "Parnell has a line on a man who might be Big Burrows. A doctor living in Radnor passed a man answering Burrows' description on the Pike the night she was murdered. The man wore a camel's hair coat, was big, dark-complexioned, and had a prominent nose. The doctor passed him at about the spot where Lucy's body was later found."

"Considering that it was dark, this doctor has made a rather remarkable identification," Wilks said. "Perhaps he even stopped and chatted with the man for a few minutes."

Bannion smiled appreciatively. Wilks watched him for a few seconds, and then he smiled, too, but there was a puzzled look in his eyes. They sat in silence for an instant, smiling as if one of them had said something funny.

"Well, what's the rest of it, Dave?" Wilks said, at last.

"Parnell tells me he checked with you on this," Bannion said, pleasantly. "I had told him, you know, that I thought Lucy Carroway might fit somehow into Tom Deery's suicide.

He called Philadelphia Homicide to see if I'd turned up anything he could connect with this big-nosed man he'd learned was on the Pike. He did talk to you, didn't he?"

"Why, yes, I believe he did," Wilks said.

Bannion grinned. "He told me you said my theories were just a pipe dream."

Wilks drummed his fingers on the arms of his chair, frowning at Bannion. They were silent for as long as thirty seconds, but Bannion was still smiling. Wilks looked at his fiddling fingers, coughed and folded his hands in his lap. "All right, I told him it was a pipe dream," he said. "What about it?"

"Why, nothing, nothing at all," Bannion said.

"Well, what do you want to see me about?" Wilks said, frowning now.

"I want to tell you what I told Parnell," Bannion said.

"What did you tell him?" Wilks said, with an impatient edge on his voice.

"I told him you were right, that it was a pipe dream," Bannion said. "I realize that now. Tom Deery, Big Burrows, just a whiff of smoke, Lieutenant. Lucy Carroway was killed by a sex fiend, probably, and the chances are a hundred to one against anyone ever nabbing that character now."

"You told him it was a pipe dream," Wilks said slowly.

Bannion said nothing. He nodded.

"That strikes me as a rather curious comment," Wilks said. "Very smart, very intelligent, but still curious."

"Coming from me it's curious, you mean."

"That's what I mean, Dave. Perhaps we should have a drink and talk this over. I'd like to feel sure we understand each other."

"I think that's a good idea."

"Excuse me." Wilks returned shortly with a bottle of bonded Bourbon and two shot glasses. "I don't think we need to bother with a chaser, eh?"

"Not with that kind of whiskey," Bannion said.

"My feeling exactly."

Bannion accepted a shot glass of whiskey and smiled at Wilks. "Here's to sunnier days," he said.

"Right," Wilks said, raising his glass.

They drank and he refilled both glasses. He sat down, the drink beside him on a table, and re-lit his pipe. "Well, I'm surprised, I must say," he said, watching Bannion with a little smile.

"You didn't think I was that smart, eh?"

Wilks laughed. "Well, that's putting it bluntly," he said. His cheeks had reddened slightly with the liquor, and his pipe made a comfortable, popping noise in the still room.

"It takes some people longer than others to learn the score," Bannion said.

"Why did you tell me this, Dave?' Wilks said, taking his pipe from his mouth.

"My reasons aren't idealistic," Bannion said. "I've got to live, that's why. I've got a daughter to take care of, too, and neither of us can get by on temperament." He shrugged. "I've got to work, Lieutenant. I thought of the private investigation field, since it's about all I know. However, I wouldn't get far without some police cooperation."

"You would have cooperation," Wilks said, picking up his drink. "You've got friends from the top to the bottom of the police department in this city. Good friends, Dave. But friendship is a give-and-take proposition. It can't be one-sided. And friendship, the kind we're talking about, is based on loyalty. I'll tell you something: You could come back to the department tomorrow if you like. Or you can establish yourself as a private investigator. And in either case you'd have friends, friends who only want to be sure of your loyalty."

"You might call Parnell, if you're not sure," Bannion said.

"I don't need to do that," Wilks said smiling. He lifted the bottle from the floor at his feet and poured two more drinks. "There's a saying, 'Once a cop always a cop', and I put stock in it. You were in the business too long to forget that, Dave." He frowned and shook his head slowly. "It was a rotten break about your wife, a dirty, rotten break. I don't blame you for blowing your top about it."

"I blew my top," Bannion said. "That's over."

"It takes a big man to see it that way."

"You have to live," Bannion said.

Wilks studied him a moment, and a hard, pleased smile

touched his lips. "I told you that once before, Dave," he said. "I told you to throw your books of philosophy away. They're full of rosy unrealities for college kids. You've learned more about life in the past three weeks, I think, than you have in the last three decades. You know now that you've got to make compromises."

"Yes, I know that now," Bannion said.

The hard smile left Wilks' face. He shook his head. "This is almost funny, Dave. You know I never liked you. Does that surprise you?"

"Well, I always thought we got along all right," Bannion said. There was an uncertain smile on his face, a puzzled little smile for Wilks' benefit, but he was thinking: Yes, you hated me, and everything else in the world which proved that corruption wasn't inevitable.

"No, I didn't like you one damn bit," Wilks said, putting down his empty glass. He was drifting into an expressive mood. "You were a little too pure for my taste, a little too sweet and innocent. And people like that get to be a nuisance, they get to be, well, critical."

"I never meant to be that way," Bannion said.

"Oh, hell, I'm rambling around miles off the topic," Wilks said, laughing, and reaching for the bottle. "What difference does it make what I thought of you last week or last year, Dave? The thing is, I like you now. Not just because you got smart, but because you're a damn big man." He stretched his legs out in front of him and laughed. "Not just physically, either."

Yes, you like me . . . I'm up to my waist in the mud with you, and we're just a pair of happy, compromising kids now. Bannion sipped his drink, and then said, "Thanks, Lieutenant."

Wilks shifted forward on the edge of his chair. "It's a relief to talk to you, Dave. You were always intelligent, and now, thank God, you're almost smart. You know we don't make all the rules. We take orders in certain cases, because it's human nature for some people to run things and other people to be run. And is there anything wrong with that? Hell, it's the story of the world. If you don't take the orders, if you decide to be a hero, does that change things? Not one damn bit. They find someone else who'd do the job, and your personal little revolt is just a waste of time. If you don't take it someone else will, by God." He glanced down at the papers at his feet and suddenly swore, angrily and fluently. "Now look at this mess they're stirring up," he said, kicking at the top front page with his foot. "Three stories there about us, about what they call our corruption and inefficiency. They're just trying to sell papers. They don't fool me. Do they think this is going to do any good? Dave, you can scream about gambling and politics until you're blue in the face, but you can't change human nature."

"I'll drink to that," Bannion said, smiling.

"What? Oh, sure. I'll have a nightcap, too." He glanced at the empty glass in surprise and then laughed. "I don't remember the last one, if you can believe it. Well, happy days."

"We can use some."

"Yes, we can use some happier days," Wilks said, sighing and rubbing his forehead. "Frankly, Dave, I don't know what's going to happen. Everything is very touchy. Damn, it's a rare night when I can get to sleep lately. It's not like the old days. The papers are after us in earnest now, and the politicians of the other party are after our heads. We've done as well as most administrations, I'd say, but reform groups are unreasonable. They want blood. It will blow over after elections, I'm sure, but right now, *before* elections, things are almighty damn tense. That's why the Deery matter was so bad and why it had to be handled so carefully." He glanced at Bannion. "You know that, don't you, Dave?"

"Sure, sure," Bannion said, looking only casually interested. It was a good act; he suddenly had an idea what Deery's suicide had meant to the city.

"They couldn't be too careful about it," Wilks said.

"Naturally."

"Then the Carroway girl started talking, and you got into it," Wilks said, shaking his head. "It was one of those nightmare things that just won't stay covered up." Wilks finished his drink, and when he put the glass down his face had changed, had smoothed over and closed. He glanced at his wrist watch smiling. "Well, time goes fast in pleasant company, doesn't it?"

Bannion knew Wilks was through talking. He had to gamble now, shoot the works behind his hunch. He said, "Deery left a note, didn't he?"

"Where'd you hear that?" Wilks said sharply.

Bannion shrugged. "It just figures. Otherwise, why all the excitement?"

"Yes, yes, of course," Wilks said, rubbing his hands together slowly.

"Was it pretty strong?"

"My God, yes. I've never seen it, but I understand it's absolute dynamite. It wasn't just a note, it was twenty typed pages of names, dates, figures——" Wilkes stopped, shrugging helplessly. "It was the works, Dave. A blueprint of the organization's structure."

"Where'd he get the dope?"

Wilks swore. "Deery was no boy scout. Until eight or ten years ago, he was in up to his neck. He collected the gambling take from the police districts throughout the city, and got his, of course. Also he set up dummy books for the amusement-tax office. Then he wanted out. Said he had his and was satisfied. Well, they let him go, they believed the bastard. And this is the way he repaid their confidence. He made records of everything—how gambling districts are lined up street by street, with police districts to avoid any misunderstandings. What captains get what, how much they keep, how much is passed on to the Inspector, the Superintendent's office. He named the judges and magistrates on Lagana's payroll, and listed what they get for continuing gambling cases indefinitely, and for handing down suspended sentences." Wilks shook his head and reached for the bottle automatically. "He went into the tax rebates, the most ticklish area in the whole damn business. Amusement-tax rebates, contractor's rebates, personal and real property rebates—you know what that could mean if it got out, Dave? He had the list of businesses owned by Lagana and Stone, and by Waxman in Central, and O'Neill in the Northeast, and how they got special city contracts and tax breaks of every kind imaginable. And anybody in the city who ever used city material in building his home—and there's a lot of those, don't think there isn't—is down there in black and white, too. Well, you can see the stink this would cause before elections? You can guess what the papers would have done with it. Well, then the Carroway girl started talking to you, and they simply couldn't afford to have any attention directed toward Deery, because if the papers got scratching around they might have turned up this business of the note."

"Well, why don't they burn the damn thing?" Bannion said.

"There's a hitch. Mrs. Deery got the note, and she's hanging onto it."

"She's an intelligent woman, isn't she?"

"Yes, yes of course. She's playing ball."

"Then, there's nothing to worry about."

"No, I suppose not, but it was a damn bad week."

"Well, it's always darkest before dawn, they say," Bannion said. He covered a yawn and smiled. "It's been a long day, hasn't it?"

They stood up and Wilks patted Bannion's big hard shoulder. "I'm glad we had this talk," he said.

"I am, too. It's meant a great deal to me," Bannion said.

"Don't worry about your plans, Dave. We can throw things your way, and don't forget it. If you need a little capital——"

Bannion waved the offer aside. "I can handle it alone, I think," he said.

Wilks came onto the front porch with him and they stood there in the quiet darkness for a few moments talking about the weather. Finally Wilks slapped his shoulder. "Well, I don't know about you, but I'm ready for bed," he said.

"You'd better get inside before you catch cold."

"Right. Goodnight, Dave."

"Goodnight, Lieutenant."

Bannion watched Wilks enter his house, watched the door close, and his face changed slowly. He stood there a moment, breathing slowly and deeply, and then he turned and went quickly down the steps, his heels ringing like iron on the dry, frozen wood . . .

Mrs. Deery stood in the doorway of her apartment, lips parted slightly, her eyebrows raised in surprise. She was ready for bed; her silver-streaked blonde hair was tied in the back with a wide blue ribbon, and her skin was oiled and shining with cold cream. "I thought you were the boy from the drugstore," she said in her low, precise voice. "I called them to send over some things I'd forgot——" She didn't complete the sentence, not from confusion, but because she obviously felt it required no further amplification.

"It's a night of coincidences, Mrs. Deery," Bannion said. "I met him outside and took over the errand." He held out a neatly wrapped package.

"Well, thank you," Mrs. Deery said, and moistened her lips.

"We don't have to worry about the boy from the drugstore now," Bannion said.

"It's rather late, you know," Mrs. Deery said.

"I want to talk to you," he said, and walked toward her slowly, hands deep in his pockets. She backed away from him, more annoyed than frightened, into the hallway of her apartment. When Bannion closed the door, she said, "You're acting very strangely, Mr. Bannion." She glanced down at the peach-colored robe, and then up at him with a prim, dramatics school expression of alarm. "I'm not dressed for company, you know."

"Don't think of me as company," Bannion said. There was a light in the living room, but the hallway and Deery's study were dark. He snapped on the hall light, and walked into Deery's study and did the same there. "Light and lust are deadly enemies, Mrs. Deery," he said. "That's from Shakespeare, the British playwright." He glanced around; the ashtray had been emptied, the typewriter covered, but nothing else had been changed.

"What do you want?" Mrs. Deery said.

"I should have seen it, of course," he said, quietly. He glanced at Mrs. Deery who stood in the doorway regarding him with lady-like exasperation. "I should have seen it because it wasn't here," he said.

"I don't know what you're talking about."

"I think you do. Tom Deery, a cautious, methodical man, shot himself in this room. His insurance policies were clipped together, his household bills were paid, his whole life was wrapped up in preparation for an orderly death. Still there was something missing—the one thing Tom Deery wouldn't have forgotten was missing."

"I think you had better go, Mr. Bannion."

"The note, that was it," Bannion said. "There had to be a note. It was inevitable, and its absence should have been instantly noticed. Tom Deery wouldn't kill himself without leaving a note to explain his reasons." He glanced at her, his face hardening. "He left a note, of course. Where is it?"

Mrs. Deery sat down on the arm of the easy chair. She looked surprised but far from shaken. "You must be a fool, Mr. Bannion," she said. "I suppose it was clever of you to find out about it, but you're certainly stupid if you think I'm going to take it from my pocket and hand it to you."

"I'll get it," Bannion said.

"Oh, no you won't," she said, in the tone she might use to deny a child's unreasonable request. "That note is my trust fund, and I'm not giving it up—to you or anyone else."

"Trust fund, eh? Then Lagana's paying you to keep it quiet."

"Certainly." Mrs. Deery swung a slippered foot slowly. "I discussed the note with him the day after Tom shot himself. He agreed to pay me a handsome amount of money, in yearly installments, if I destroyed the note."

"And you did?"

"Of course not. That would have been silly. When I talked with him the note was already in my safety deposit box, with a letter to my lawyer asking him to deliver it to the Director of Public Safety, in the presence of the press, in the event of my murder." She smiled slightly. "The note is not only a trust fund but an insurance policy, you see. Mr. Lagana will make sure that nothing happens to me."

"And you told Lagana about Lucy Carroway, I suppose."

"Why, certainly. You intimated she might know more than she had already told you. That worried Mr. Lagana. Perhaps Tom had told her about the note he was writing or planned to write. She might keep talking, and that was very dangerous, Mr. Lagana thought."

"So she was tortured to find out what she knew, and then she was murdered," Bannion said. "You've got a lot on your soul, Mrs. Deery."

"I'm not worrying about it," Mrs. Deery said smiling. "I had no affection for Lucy Carroway. Do you think it's pleasant to realize that such a person is having an affair with your husband? I can tell you it isn't. I hated her, quite frankly, and I have no tears for her now. But I'm no ghoul. I'm sorry her end was so unpleasant."

"You're lying. You're delighted at what happened to her."

"You have a horrid mind," she said, smiling up at him, her eyes wide and bright. "Poor Lucy. What a ghastly finish to her shabby little life."

"You wouldn't have it any other way," Bannion said.

She smiled ruefully, as if caught in a small deceit. "You're right, I believe. I've saved the newspaper stories about it, and re-reading them satisfies something deep inside me, Mr. Bannion. Something not very nice, I'm afraid. But then I'm not a nice person. I'm glad she got paid off fittingly."

"You were also glad that your husband blew his brains out," Bannion said. "And you were glad to find the note. The note he left to make amends for what he had done. You denied him that chance, again quite happily, I'm sure."

"Oh, Tom was a fool," Mrs. Deery said, shrugging. "I have no sympathy with death-bed confessions. He was no angel. He was smart. He made enough for us to live decently —at first. He had soul-struggles about it, and finally decided to live on his salary. He never cared about me, of course. He didn't care that I had no clothes, no jewels, none of the things a woman might expect out of life. It was after his affair with Lucy Carroway that he turned over a new leaf, and isn't that a ridiculous development, by the way? Imagine anyone seeing the light through an association with that tramp! At any rate, like all men who've been tied to their mother's knee, he suddenly turned back to religion when he lost his nerve. Oh, he got very religious and saintly, Mr. Bannion. He spent eight years worrying about his sins, and finally he decided to absolve himself by 'telling all' in a note and blowing his brains out." She smiled contemptuously. "Fortunately, I got the note instead of the papers."

"And you'll hang onto it," Bannion said slowly. "A whole city is dying in the hands of a gang of thieves, but you don't care a bit. You'll protect Stone and Lagana, you'll save murderers from the chair, you'll let justice be kicked into the alley, just for the sake of a mink coat and a diamond brooch."

Mrs. Deery laughed softly, and then wet her lips with the tip of her small, pink tongue. "Go on, Mr. Bannion, you're really amusing," she said.

"And you'll cheat your husband out of his last chance to ease his conscience," Bannion said, in the same slow hard voice.

"Yes, yes, yes," Mrs. Deery said, snapping the words out fiercely. "I've suffered, and now it's over. I'm going to enjoy life to the hilt now, and none of your dreary moralizing affects me in the least."

"You think the coming years are going to be good?"

She seemed amused at the question. "Certainly, I do."

"You're wrong."

"They'll be wonderful years," Mrs. Deery said, and began to laugh.

"There aren't going to be any years at all," Bannion said slowly.

"What do you mean?"

Bannion's face was hard and gray as he took the gun from his shoulder holster. "Can't you guess, Mrs. Deery?"

"—You won't do it."

"The note will be delivered, then," Bannion said. "The note with the papers present. That's the big heat, bright lady. For Lagana, Stone, the rest of our city's thieving bastards."

Mrs. Deery slid from the arm of the chair in one fluid, slack movement, and went to her knees before Bannion. She looked up at him, moving her body slowly from side to side, and wetting her pale lips with her tongue. Her mouth opened and closed, her hands made fluttering gestures to accompany the words; but no words sounded.

She knelt before him, grotesquely, ludicrously, her expression changing, twisting, registering all the variations of appeal, fear, terror, pity, in an attempt to match those silent words that were sounding only in her mind. It was a pantomime of terror, cajolery, a deaf-mute's frantic plea of pity.

This was the end of it, Bannion thought, seeing her as only the last obstacle between him and vengeance. When the shot sounded, when this mute, foolishly gesticulating creature was dead, he could put his gun away and call the police. The job would be done.

"No!" Mrs. Deery managed the one hoarse word.

Why did he wait? He had only to pull the trigger, let the firing pin snap forward, and the steel-jacketed bullet would take care of the rest, take care of this soft, perfumed, sadistic bitch, and with her Stone, Lagana, the hoodlums who had murdered his wife and held this town in their big, bitter grip.

"I can pay you," Mrs. Deery cried.

Why did he wait? They had killed, why shouldn't he? They had murdered Lucy Carroway, Kate, his life and love, as they'd destroy bothersome insects. Why should he bind himself with morals which they had mocked?

Mrs. Deery stared at him, whimpering now, her mouth working loosely.

Bannion's arm came down slowly until the muzzle of the gun pointed at the floor. "I don't have the right to kill you," he said, in a low, raging voice.

She put her hands to her face, sobbing, and leaned forward until her forehead rested on Bannion's shoe. He jerked his foot away savagely, and she slumped to the floor, laughing and crying at the same time, her hand stroking the rug in a slow, loving caress.

Bannion looked down at her without expression and put his gun away. He shrugged then, a gesture of immense and bitter weariness, and walked out of her apartment. The sound of her low, wild, grateful weeping followed him to his car.

Sixteen

BANNION STOPPED AT the first bar he saw and ordered a whiskey. It didn't touch the coldness inside him. Now he had to start all over, do it the clean way. Force the note into the open, by pressure or cleverness, but not by shooting a helpless woman. He wasn't as hard as he'd thought; the oath he'd sworn to Kate was just a loud, empty word.

He had another drink and then went to the telephone booth and called Debby.

"Everything okay?" he said when she answered.

"Sure. Shouldn't it be?"

"I don't know. One of Stone's men, I think, was at the hotel asking for you this evening. He knows where you are, obviously."

"What should I do, Bannion?"

He rubbed his forehead. He didn't know and didn't care.

"Why don't you say it?" she said, laughing shakily. "I'm just a millstone around your neck. I know it, Bannion."

"Stop it," he said irritably.

"All right, I'll stop it."

"That's better."

"How did your lead turn out?"

He sighed. "A dead-end street. This will be Greek to you, but one of our city's finest left a note and then blew a hole through his head. The note will do what I may never be able to do to Lagana and company. It will be his end. However, Deery's wife has the note now, and I wasn't tough enough to bend to the Fifth Commandment even a little bit. If I had—well that's another story. Don't worry about it, Debby. There'll be another chance."

"You sound cryptic, if that's the right word," Debby said.

"Don't worry about it," he said. He had talked only to relieve the pressure inside him, but it hadn't helped.

"Okay, I won't. But what should I do, Bannion? I don't want to be picked up by Stone."

"Sit tight, I'll be along pretty soon."

"I'll be waiting for you. It doesn't mean anything, but I miss you."

"I'll be along soon," he said. He walked back to the bar and ordered another drink.

Larry Smith looked down at the green runway lights as the plane banked into its base-leg circuit of the field. It was nighttime and the rows of parallel lights stretched into a black infinity, mysterious but comforting symbols of order and safety.

Pittsburgh, first stop on the coast flight.

He shouldn't have run out, Larry told himself hopelessly, despairingly, for about the fiftieth time. Lagana and Stone would have understood. You didn't keep your mouth shut when a man like Bannion had his hands on your throat and was ready to crush the life from your body. No, you talked. Anyone would. They'd understand that. But he shouldn't have run. That looked bad . . .

He remembered Lagana's eyes and shuddered. The interior of the plane was warm and dim, a strange little haven of safety and comfort, but Larry shuddered . . .

Max Stone paced the floor of his living room, chewing on an unlit cigar and trying to keep his rage in check. Art Keene stood beside the liquor cabinet, watching him with no expression at all on his lean, blank face. Occasionally Stone glared at the two men who sat miserably together on the couch. Once he yelled at them, "Punks, that's all you are."

"I don't think it was their fault," Art Keene said.

"Well, don't bother thinking so much," Stone said, taking the cigar from his mouth and staring at Keene.

Keene shrugged and didn't answer.

It was nearly midnight, and Stone wore a red silk bathrobe and pajamas. The day in bed had helped his hangover, but with the physical improvement had come an immense need for action. The city was going to hell, he knew; and he wanted to do something about it, anything, as long as it was fast, violent and effective. Take the bastards causing trouble and slap them down hard. That's what he wanted to do, but Lagana said no, and the old man meant it.

The knock he was expecting sounded, and Stone hurried to the door. Lagana came in, frowning, the big man named Gordon on his heels.

"Okay, what happened this time?" he said, in a low, disgusted voice. He glanced around the room, stripping off his gloves. The two men on the couch seemed to shrink under his eyes, and Art Keene busied himself lighting a cigarette.

Stone glared at the men on the couch, too. "Why don't you surprise us by doing something right, you punks?" he yelled.

The man called Creamy moistened his big, slack mouth. There was a cut over his forehead, a streak of dried blood on his cheek, and his eyelids were blinking rapidly, as if he was trying to hold back tears. The man beside him, Danielbaum, was in worse shape. Two of his front teeth were out, and his lips were bruised and swollen. There was a quality of hysteria in his bright nervous smile, his darting eyes, the erratic jerks and twitches of his body.

"You shouldn't say that, Max," he said, grimacing, tapping the floor with a nervous foot. "Those guys damn near killed us. There were eight or ten of them, and——"

"The numbers are going up every minute," Stone said.

"All right, let's have the story," Lagana said, staring at Danielbaum.

Creamy began to cry. Danielbaum wet his lips, his eyes bright and senseless with fear. "We did our best, we did our best, Mr. Lagana. You see, we were going to deliver the warrants, and——"

"Stone told me about that," Lagana said, cutting him off

with an impatient wave of his hand. "What happened when
you got there?"

"Well, we saw a cop out in front, and I recognized him as
Cranston," Danielbaum went on as Creamy continued to provide a sniffling counterpoint to the story. "I thought it was
just a coincidence, maybe, so we went around to the back.
That's where this queer jumped us, an Indian he was. Then a
bunch of guys piled out of the house. They tore the warrants
up and started to work us over."

"Were they cops?" Lagana said.

"No, they must have been an out-of-town mob," Danielbaum said, twitching nervously. "Mr. Lagana, they were
hard. They had guns and they acted like they grew up with 'em
in their fists."

Lagana paced up and down the floor slowly, a worried little
line appearing over his eyes. "But they let you go, eh?"

Creamy and Danielbaum nodded.

"I should of sent a couple of Boy Scouts," Stone said.

"Did you call the district on this?" Lagana said to Stone.

"Yeah. They're sending a car over to look into it. I told the
sergeant to lock up everybody he found there."

"How long ago was that?"

"Half hour, forty-five minutes."

"Well, they may know something by now," Lagana said.
He went to the phone and put a call through the Police Board
to the district. "This is Mike Lagana," he said, when the connection was made. His voice was low and pleasant. "Who's
talking, by the way?"

"Sergeant Diamond, Mr. Lagana."

"Sorry to bother you, Sergeant, but what have you heard
about a complaint that was made about half an hour ago,
something about some private citizens in your district resisting
and mauling a couple of constables?"

"The car got back a few minutes ago, Mr. Lagana."

"I see. What's the story?"

"Well, the officers say there was just a bunch of fellows sitting around playing poker. Nothing to the complaint, I
guess."

"There was something to the complaint," Lagana said, in a
harder voice. "I'm telling you so, Sergeant. You send a car

back there and pick up everyone in that poker game."

"Mr. Lagana, there was a police Inspector sitting in that game, and a priest from Saint Gertrude's. I'm not going to arrest them, unless I get an order from the Superintendent." The Sergeant wasn't defiant; but he wasn't afraid.

"You know who you're talking to?" Lagana said, surprised.

"Yes, sir, Mr. Lagana, but I——"

Lagana put the phone down with a crash. "Bannion's getting cute," he said, slapping his gloves down against his open palm. He frowned at the floor for a moment, and then, automatically, he checked the pulse in his left wrist. His lips moved, counting, but still he frowned at the floor, apparently unaware of what he was doing. "I don't like this very much," he said, at last. "However, we won't do anything about it. Not right now." He put his hands in his pockets and squared his shoulders. "What about Larry?" he said, glancing at Stone.

Stone looked at Keene. "Where'd you say he went?"

"He bought a through ticket to Los Angeles."

"Well, we've got some friends out there," Lagana said, thoughtfully. "Give them a call, Max, and tell them friend Larry is a loudmouth."

"Sure thing."

"Come on, Gordon, let's go," Lagana said. "I'm tired."

Watching him go, seeing the slow step, the strangely gray face, Stone felt an uneasy stab of fear. The old man was worried, and that wasn't like him. He always said people worried because they couldn't think. But he was worrying now; maybe it was the time when thinking wasn't any good. Maybe it was time to worry.

"Let's have a drink," Stone said. He glanced at Creamy and Danielbaum, aware that he was frowning. "Well, don't look so sad," he said. "Everybody makes mistakes."

Bannion parked before his hotel, checking the street with a quick glance, and walked into the lobby. The night clerk gave him his key, and said, "That girl you took a room for has gone, Mr. Bannion."

"Was she alone?"

"Yes, she was alone."

"I see." Bannion lit a cigarette, feeling oddly let down. "Did she leave any message?"

"Why, yes. She just asked me to tell you she wouldn't be back."

"I see, thanks." Well, that was that. She might have gone to Stone, although it wasn't likely. Probably she was on the run. He wondered if she had any money . . .

Bannion went up to his room and made himself a drink. He stretched out on the bed, lit a cigarette and stared at the ceiling. The faint night sounds of traffic, a man's laugh, a train starting up, drifted in on him with a curiously depressing effect . . .

The phone at his elbow rang. Bannion lifted the receiver and said, "Yes?"

"Bannion?"

He knew the voice. "Yes. Where are you?"

"I decided to get out of your hair," she said. "You were a good egg about it, but I was a nuisance." She laughed then, an odd little laugh. "You weren't so tough after all. But that's okay. You're better off being a little soft."

"Are you all right?" he said.

"Sure, I'm fine."

"Where are you?"

"Did I forget that? I'm at Mrs. Deery's, Bannion."

Bannion sat up abruptly. "Are you crazy? What in hell are you doing there?"

"I'm proving something, I guess." She laughed again, softly. "I'm proving I'm a tough guy."

"Get the hell out of there, Debby."

"No, I'm staying."

Bannion hesitated, feeling a sudden coldness in his stomach. "Where's Mrs. Deery, Debby?"

"She's dead, Bannion."

"You're crazy."

"Maybe. Anyway, I'm a tough guy. I did what you couldn't do, Bannion. I did it for both of us."

"Debby, you're out of your mind. You didn't do a damn thing for me."

"Well, I like to think I did. It's nice to think that. Give a girl that much, Bannion."

"This is a gag, a stupid, silly gag."

"No, it's no gag. I read the papers, you know, and I read about Deery. That's why I came out here. He left a note, and his wife had it. You were do damn cryptic, if that's the word I mean. About not being strong enough to bend the Fifth Commandment." She laughed, a high, happy laugh. "You must have thought I never went to Sunday School with all the good little girls. You thought I wouldn't get it, eh?"

"Debby, listen to me!"

"Not now, Bannion. She had the note, and you couldn't kill her. Well, I could. It was easy. With the little gun Stone gave me to protect myself in this big bad city. He's through now, isn't he? When the note comes out, he'll be through, won't he?"

Bannion got to his feet, reaching for his coat with his free hand. "Listen Debby! Sit tight, I'm coming out there. You wait for me, do you hear?"

"No, I can't wait Bannion. Goodbye, you big baby. You were nice to me, so thanks."

The phone clicked in his ear. Bannion jiggled the hook several times, and then looked up the Deery number in the phone book. He tried it but got no answer.

Bannion paced the floor, frowning, rubbing his big hands together slowly. Finally he stopped and sat down at the phone. He hesitated again, then called the *Express,* and got Jerry Furnham's home number . . .

Furnham sounded as if he had been asleep.

"Jerry, this is Dave Bannion. I've got what may be a good story." He talked rapidly for half a minute, and when he stopped, Furnham said, "I'll get right on it, Dave." He didn't sound sleepy now. "We can find that lawyer. If this is straight, the lid's going off. Thanks."

Bannion picked up his hat and coat and left the room.

Seventeen

THE NEWS SPREAD slowly, almost casually at first, from one cop to another, from a police captain to a magistrate, and then it picked up speed and flew through the night, from the top to the bottom, from one end of the city to the other. Telephones rang shrilly. Lights went on in homes on the Main Line, in downtown hotels, in homes and apartments in all sections of the city. Men with suddenly stricken faces looked at worried wives, or bored, sleepy girls, and then some of them took sedatives and others took stimulants, and a few began packing bags and checking plane and train schedules. The lucky ones, the great honest majority, grinned at the news and went back to bed with the pleasant realization that heads would be rolling by tomorrow night.

The big heat was coming . . .

At nine-thirty the following morning a lawyer named William Copelli walked into the Director of Public Safety's office on the fourth floor of the Hall. Counselor Copelli was a thin balding man in his early forties, with quick eyes and an earnest, school-teacherish expression. He was slightly nervous, and kept clearing his throat with short, barking coughs. There were six reporters and three photographers at the lawyer's heels.

Standing beside the Director's desk was Inspector Cranston, clean-shaven, well-rested, buttons and braid shining. There was just the trace of a smile on his straight, hard mouth as he nodded to the newspapermen. He had been appointed Acting Superintendent of police at nine o'clock that morning. That had been the Hall's reaction to Deery's note. Reform was in the air, and they were beating the papers to the punch by putting Cranston in charge of the police department. When things cooled off they might ease him back to the Sunshine Detail. Cranston knew this, of course, and that accounted for the little smile on his hard old mouth.

The Director, a tired, graying man, announced Cranston's appointment to the reporters, and then glanced at Counselor Copelli. "What was it you wanted to see me about?" he said, with a little sigh.

The lawyer opened his briefcase and removed a sheaf of typed papers. "My late client, Mrs. Agnes Deery, requested that I read this statement in your presence, Mr. Director," he said, in a voice which grew a bit stronger with each word. "Agnes Deery, who was shot and killed last night, wanted this document to be made public in the event of her murder." Copelli cleared his throat sharply, and pulled the knot of his tie down from his prominent Adam's apple. "This statement was written by her late husband, Thomas Deery, some time before he committed suicide. Mrs. Deery stipulated that if it were impossible to read this in your presence, then copies of it should be sent to all the newspapers in the city, to the Mayor, and to the President of the City Council. However, since you've granted me the opportunity to fulfill Mrs. Deery's first request, I shall commence the reading of her husband's statement at this time."

"Please read it, Counselor," the Director said, with an uneasy sigh.

Copelli cleared his throat once more, and the reporters crowded closer to him, copy paper and pencils ready. A flash bulb exploded.

"Hold that for a while," the Director said, as Copelli started nervously. "Let's wait until he's through for the pictures."

"Thank you," Copelli said. He glanced once at the Director, and then began reading Thomas Francis Deery's suicide note in a clear, firm voice . . .

Forty-five minutes later, Copelli had finished, the Director had made a statement ("This must be looked into, of course"), and the reporters were trying to get quotes from Cranston. He waved a hand for silence, and he was no longer smiling.

"Just settle down now, boys," he said. "This isn't going to be any Roman Holiday, so get that out of your heads. Don't expect miracles. Put that in your papers. When the public interest has been sold out for decades you can't clean things up in a day—or a year, for that matter. But I'll tell you what you *can* do in one day—you can start! And today is the day we're starting." He glanced around the room, his face as hard and bright as a well-worn shield. "What we've heard isn't evidence. They are accusations, well-founded ones it appears, against the top officers of this city. Maybe it's all true; maybe only a half, or a fifth of it is true. Our job is to find out. My recommendation to the Mayor will be for a Special Grand Jury, and a special prosecutor to be appointed by the Governor in Harrisburg. And let me say once more, don't expect miracles. You won't wake up tomorrow and find yourself living in a clean, well-run city. That takes time and will. We've got to shake off a lot of bad habits. Corruption has a way of ruining everything it touches. The people of a city are corrupted, too. Instead of using their privilege as voters to fire the bastards who sell out their interests, they shrug and say, 'Well, what can you do about it?' or, 'Well, that's human nature, I guess.' Human nature, my foot. That's the voter's apology for his own laziness. Okay, that's all I've got to say." Cranston smiled slightly. "I could have saved time by saying I'm going to do what I've always done as a cop: Arrest people who break the laws."

"How about horse rooms?" a reporter said.

Inspector Cranston glanced at his watch. "Well, if you want to make a last sentimental bet, or take one more crack at your bookies, you've got just another hour. I'll buy a drink for the man who can find a handbook open in this town by noon today. That's all boys. Clear out now, we've got work to do."

They charged out then and down the hall to the phones . . .

*   *   *

Bannion sat in the white, sterile waiting room, his big hands folded in his lap, and stared down at the black-and-white linoleum floor. Trim, busy nurses went past him soundlessly on rubber-soled shoes, giving him only a quick, perfunctory glance; he had been waiting there all night, ever since the girl named Debby Something-or-other had been brought in, and he was as much a fixture now as the wicker furniture, the pictures on the walls.

It was ten-thirty in the morning when a tired, exasperated doctor came in, and said, "Well, Mr. Bannion. I don't think you can see her yet."

"How is she?"

The doctor shook his head. "We can't do much for her, I'm afraid. She's hemorrhaging internally, and we haven't been able to stop it. That often happens when people try to shoot themselves in the heart. They miss and make a mess of it. Damn, wouldn't you think people would know where their hearts are?"

"Yes, I suppose you would," Bannion said, and something in his voice made the doctor slightly uncomfortable. "When can I see her?"

"Well, that's hard to say. She's resting now. Maybe in a couple of hours, maybe tomorrow morning."

"Okay, I'll be back," Bannion said.

"Say, what did she shoot that Deery woman for?" the doctor said.

"She was doing me a favor," Bannion said. "You, too. And everybody else who lives in the city."

The doctor didn't get it, but something in Bannion's voice decided him against pressing the point. Also, he was a busy man and he didn't have too much time to spend on young blondes who tried to shoot themselves in the heart and missed . . .

It was nearly four o'clock when Bannion got to the Hall. He went up to Cranston's office and found the old man alone at his desk.

"Well, I was just about to send out the alarm for you," Cranston said.

Bannion sat down and pushed his hat back on his forehead.

"What's been going on?" he said.

"You didn't look at a paper?"

"No, I was busy."

"Well, so were we. It was a very profitable day, thanks to you, Dave."

"That's good. What about the big boys? Lagana and Stone?"

"We won't have to worry about Lagana, Dave."

"Why not?"

"He's dead."

Bannion shrugged tiredly. "You might know he'd cop an out. Well, the suckers in hell can get some action tonight. What happened?"

"He got the news of Deery's note last night. He worked at his desk all night, making calls, trying to find out how bad it was, I imagine. This morning he lay down to rest. Wasn't feeling too well, his wife said. He never woke up."

"Heart, eh?"

"That's what the doctor said."

Bannion looked over Cranston's head and out at the city brightening to nighttime life now as the street lights went on, and automobile headlights cut through the gray gloom of the streets.

"So he's dead, eh?" he said. "That leaves the organization."

"It will die, too. If they leave me here for six months, if the public stays awake, it will die. Take a look at the papers. The Ins don't have a chance in the elections. Some honest men are coming, and by God it's about time. Deery's note was the bombshell, all right. You can take a bow, Dave."

"Thanks."

Cranston raised his eyebrows. "You did it alone, didn't you?"

"I thought so at first," Bannion said. "Lonely figure against the mob. That wasn't it, Inspector. I had help, all I could use. From Lucy Carroway, from a detective in Radnor named Parnell, from you and Burke, and from a colored woman in Chester." He shrugged, smiling slightly. "And there were some GI friends of mine, and a priest and a girl named Debby. Hell, Inspector, I had a mob with me. All the decent people in the city, I guess.''

"I'm glad you see that," Cranston said.

"Where's Stone, by the way?"

"We haven't located him yet. We have no reason to pick him up, but I want to keep a line on him. We need a warrant and an indictment first. We'll get them, and we don't move until we do." There was a slight, unmistakable edge in his voice, and he met Bannion's eyes squarely. "This is going to be legal, remember, Dave."

"Why sure," Bannion said. "He's your baby."

"Well, keep that in mind."

Bannion smiled; his casual tone hadn't fooled the old man. "Be sure you get him, Inspector."

"I'll get him, don't you worry."

Bannion stood up and they shook hands. "Get some sleep, Dave," Cranston said.

"I've got nothing else on my mind. Goodnight, Inspector," Bannion said.

Cranston watched him leave, and then he sat down and put in a call to Homicide. "I want to talk to Detective Burke," he said.

He was frowning.

Eighteen

STONE ENTERED HIS apartment at eleven o'clock that night. He switched on the overhead lights, all the floor lamps, and then shouted for Alex. The room was cold, he thought, rubbing his hands together and pacing restlessly.

Alex came hurrying in, and Stone laughed at the look in his face. "Well, what's wrong with you," he said, taking a queer pleasure from the man's fear.

"Nothing, nothing, Max. It's just—just that everything's up in the air."

"That's a lot of Sunday School talk in the Hall," Stone said. He had spent the day winding up a few deals, and making arrangements to transfer his cash assets to banks in Detroit, Chicago and Los Angeles. It had been one nightmare after another all day long; Lagana's death coming right after Deery's statement had been a terrible jolt. Everything was slipping: Lagana was dead, and Cranston had the city in his hands.

"I want a drink, a double Scotch," he told Alex. "Then pack me a bag and take it down to the car. Well, get going, damn it."

Stone felt better after the drink. He checked his plane tickets, his cash and the gun in the pocket of his overcoat. This was the time for a vacation, a nice, long one. After about six months of sun, say, he could come back and knock down any indictments or warrants that had been issued for him or his friends. Art Keene was staying; he was a damn fool. Keene thought the heat would be off in a week, but Stone knew otherwise; this was the big blast and it was going to stick for a while.

Alex came in and told him the bag was down in the car.

"Good," Stone said. "Now listen: I'm taking a plane trip. I'll leave the car at the field, in the parking lot with the keys in the glove compartment. You pick it up tomorrow morning. Give it to Jerry at the garage, and tell him to put it on blocks. If anybody wants me you tell 'em I went up to Maine to do some fishing. Got all that?"

"Sure, Max, sure. Am I supposed to know when you're coming back?"

"Yeah, I'll be back next week."

"This trouble is bad, isn't it?"

"Stop stewing. It will be over in a month."

"But everybody's scared, Max. Judge McGraw killed himself, I read."

"He was always a weak sister. Do I look scared?" Stone laughed at Alex. "Take a drink and warm up, for God's sake. So long, I'll see you next week."

He took the service elevator down to the garage. He unwrapped a cigar, and lit it, listening to the steady, reassuring hum of the elevator cables. He was relieved to be on his way.

The elevator came to rest with a soft jar. Stone let himself out and snapped on the lights in the garage. He walked to the corrugated iron doors, punched a wall button, and watched them roll smoothly up and out of the way. It was a cold night, with a light rain falling. Stone glanced up at the sky. It was probably okay for flying, he thought.

He turned back into the garage and his heart gave a sudden, uneven lurch.

There was a man standing beside his car, a huge man in a wet trenchcoat, a man with a pale, tired, merciless face. It was Bannion, Stone saw, and slowly, casually, he let his hands slip into the slash pocket of his coat.

"Taking a trip, eh?" Bannion said.

"Anything wrong with that?"

"It may disappoint Inspector Cranston. He's thinking about arresting you next month, or maybe it's next year. Depends on how long it will take to do it legally."

"I don't make plans that far in advance," Stone said. "If he's going to arrest me let him do it tonight." His hand touched the gun in his pocket. He must slip his fingers around the butt, get one over the trigger, bring the muzzle up and shoot through his coat—without letting Bannion see what was coming. Stone wet his lips. He had eaten hurriedly today and had drunk a lot, and his stomach was burning painfully. He could taste the last drink he'd had, and, underneath that, something else, something dry and harsh and cold.

"You're not going anywhere," Bannion said. "I can't wait for Cranston to make it legal. I don't make plans that far in advance either."

Stone wet his lips, tasting again the cold, dry harshness beneath the last drink. "You're making a mistake, Bannion," he said, and his hand closed over the gun in his pocket.

Bannion laughed. "All right, you've got the gun in your hand now, Stone. Go ahead and shoot. Think of my wife while you're shooting."

"You sonofabitch," Stone shouted, and twisted the gun up to cover Bannion. "Now you get yours."

"I'm waiting," Bannion said.

Stone backed slowly into the alley, wetting his lips, moving his legs with great effort, and trying desperately to close his finger down against the trigger. Something was welling in him, washing away his strength; he heard his stomach churning, and felt fear running like an electric current through his arms and legs. Sweat broke out on his face. "I'll kill you," he shouted, but his voice was pitifully weak in his ears. The wind seemed to tear it from his mouth and carry it away down the dark alley. Bannion was coming toward him slowly. He saw the overhead light in the garage touch the detective's cold, hard face, and heard his footsteps strike the concrete with a deliberate, measured tread.

"No, you aren't killing anybody else," Bannion said.

"Don't come any closer," Stone shouted. "I've got guys to

take care of you. I'll put in a call. I'll turn on the heat, you stinking cop.''

Bannion laughed.

Another voice said calmly, "Get your hands out of your pockets, Stone. You're under arrest."

Bannion moved swiftly to one side, and a gun appeared almost magically in his hands. Stone wheeled to the new voice, and a little cry of terror broke from his lips. He saw a shadowy figure at the side of the garage, and the blur of a lean, pale face. Suddenly his strength returned; this was just another cop, a fifty-dollar-a-week slob, a chump to be jerked around on the end of a string. He almost sobbed with relief. This was a thing he could handle; this wasn't Bannion.

"Don't be a sucker," he shouted at the man who stood in the shadows.

"You're under arrest, Stone," the man said.

Stone laughed, and swung around. He fired twice at the voice, and felt the bullets rip through his coat. His hand, holding the gun awkwardly, twisted under the recoil. A blue-orange flash exploded in the darkness, and Stone felt a bullet strike his stomach, and another his chest, but for an instant his mind was clear and untouched, and he marveled that there was no pain, no sensation at all, only the solid, jarring impact of the bullets.

He tried to squeeze the trigger once more, knowing with a giddy illogical relief that it wasn't Bannion who had shot him, but the pain hit him then, sharply, sickeningly, and he forgot Bannion, forgot everything, and began to scream. Stumbling into the alley, he turned and ran toward the intersection, bent over, hobbling like a drunk and shouting with wild, fierce anger.

Bannion stepped out of the garage and saw Burke standing in the shadows, a gun in his hand. The two men looked at each other for a few seconds without speaking, and then they put their guns away, and walked down the alley, their shoulders nearly touching, following the sound of Stone's voice.

Stone stopped at the intersection. This wasn't happening to him, not to Max Stone. He wasn't running through the night, screaming, tasting blood in his throat. He coughed and began to strangle. There was nothing to do but run, run from the pain, the hoarse bellowing of his own voice, from the man named Bannion. Somebody must take care of Bannion. Stone shouted orders; he must have help.

He reached Walnut Street and stopped at the corner, clinging weakly to a street lamp. The street was empty. Rain glistened on the car tracks, and the tracks stretched out to infinity. He shouted again, sobbing, and his voice was the only sound in the silence.

He looked around wildly. Bannion was coming after him, walking slowly, hands lost in the pockets of his trenchcoat, his gray, merciless face shadowed by the brim of his hat.

Stone turned and ran, but his legs gave way and he crashed to his knees. He tried to think, plan, but a river of pain washed through his mind, washing his thoughts and plans into darkness.

Watching, Bannion saw him climb jerkily to his feet and raise his hands high above his head. Stone was still shouting wildly, and his shadow, grotesque and menacing, fell across the city. But when he staggered and toppled to the wet pavement, the shadow shortened with a rush, contracted magically to the small and unimportant size of a dead man lying in a gutter.

Bannion stood in the yellow glow of the street lamp staring down at Stone's body. He rubbed his forehead tiredly, thinking, now it's over, over at last. He had lived with anger and sadness for an eternity, it seemed. Now the anger was gone, and there was nothing left but the sadness. For himself, for everyone, even a reluctant bit of it for Max Stone.

Burke said, "Cranston wasn't fooled, Dave. He knew you were after Stone."

"Cranston's smart," Bannion said.

"He told me to pick him up," Burke said.

"It didn't work out that way."

Burke shrugged, "Just as well."

A crowd was forming. A street car had stopped, and the motorman was in the street, and from Stone's building two uniformed bellboys were hurrying to the scene. People were trotting along the sidewalks, their footsteps sharp and excited in the cold night.

"All right, all right," Burke said, walking up to Stone's body. "This is police business, folks. Don't hang around blocking traffic. Go on home, go on home . . ."

Bannion watched him for a few seconds and then turned and walked slowly away, his hands buried deep in the pockets of his trenchcoat.

Nineteen

THERE WAS ANOTHER doctor on duty now, and he told Bannion it would be all right for him to see Debby. "You might just as well," he said, as they walked along the silent, tile-floored corridor. "I don't think it will make much difference." He opened the door of Debby's room, and went on about his work.

Bannion walked to the side of her bed, and she turned her head to him and smiled. They had changed the bandage on her face, and someone, a nurse, Bannion supposed, had combed her hair. She looked desperately tired; there were purple hollows under her eyes, and her skin was transparently white.

"How are you feeling?" he said.

"Oh, fine," she said, in a low soft voice. "Sit down, Bannion. Can you stay a little while?"

"Sure, of course," he said, and sat down in the straight-backed chair beside her bed. "You look pretty good, considering the excitement you've been through."

"I feel all right," she said. "I shouldn't have done it, Bannion. I shouldn't have shot her. I did it to get Stone, but it was wrong."

"Well, let's don't talk about it now," he said.

"You never want to talk," she said, and turned her face to the wall. They were silent for a few moments. Bannion noticed a soft, early dawn light at the windows. It would go away after

180

a few minutes, and return strongly in an hour or so, he knew.

"I felt I was doing right," Debby said. "Stone shouldn't have ruined my looks. It was a terrible thing for him to do. A girl with only looks to keep her from being a bum can't afford to lose them. And it hurts worse when you don't have anything else. Maybe it wouldn't be so bad for someone with a family and kids, or an education even, but I didn't have those things. I thought it was right to pay him back, but I shouldn't have killed her, Bannion."

"It's all over now," he said.

"Don't do anything to Stone," she said, looking at him, and shaking her head slowly, tiredly. He saw that she was near tears. "Don't mess yourself up, Bannion. Let him alone. Let the police take care of him."

"Okay, Debby," he said.

"It's not worth it. It's all bad, this hating people." She wet her lips. "Am I going to die?"

"—I don't know, Debby. You look in good shape."

"Oh, I'm in great shape."

They didn't talk much for a while. Debby turned her face aside and Bannion sat there, feeling the need for sleep in his eyes, and watched her slim, pale hands. He sat quietly, watching her hands, as the dawn slanted slowly into the room. The nurse was in and out, and came back with the doctor. They moved around her quietly, adjusting her pillow, checking her pulse. The doctor caught Bannion's eye and shook his head slowly.

"Should I go?" Bannion said.

"No, you might as well stay."

Debby turned her head. "Bannion, why aren't we talking? We're sitting here like bumps on a log." Her voice was so low that he had to lean forward to catch what she said.

"Okay, we'll talk then," he said.

The nurse and doctor left quietly.

"You were mad when I asked you about your wife," she said. "You thought I wasn't good enough to know about her, didn't you?"

"Don't be ridiculous," Bannion said. He tried to laugh casually.

"No, I knew what you meant."

"You're being silly. My wife's name was Kate. You and she would have got along pretty well, I think."

"Yeah? What was she like?"

Bannion swallowed the sudden dryness in his throat. "Well, she had quite a temper for one thing. She was a genuine Irish blow-top, if you know the type. Fortunately, she got over it in a hurry. She couldn't stay mad very long. She'd raise hell with me for missing dinner, or leaving the bathroom in a mess, and five minutes later she'd bring me a drink as if nothing had happened."

"That's the best way to be," Debby said. "Why hold grudges?" She smiled at him and her voice was drowsy.

Bannion picked up one of her thin hands, and wondered if he should call the doctor. "She used to get impatient with the baby, too," he said. "I don't think Brigid really minded though." He wet his lips. "She was shrewd enough to work through me when she was in the dog-house with Kate. She's just four, but she's already got the makings of a politician."

"You've got a little girl," Debby said.

"Yes, and she's quite a person." He tried to put a smile in his voice. "When I worked days Kate would have her dressed up like a queen when I got home. I suppose it's the same in most families, but that was a big moment for me, to walk in and see her looking like something that had climbed down from a birthday cake."

"That must have been nice," Debby said, and sighed. "I'm glad you told me about her, Bannion." She didn't say anything else; she turned her head to one side and closed her eyes. Bannion was still holding her hand when the doctor came in, checked her pulse and told him that she was dead.

Bannion got stiffly to his feet. "I might as well go then," he said. "See about an undertaker, will you please? There'll be money for it."

"Yes, of course."

"Thanks, Doctor."

Bannion came out of the hospital into the cold, still, purple gray light of dawn. He stood on the sidewalk for a few moments, breathing deeply, and then he turned and walked slowly toward the center of the city.

There were garbage cans at the curb, and a rubber-tired

milk wagon ahead of him in the next block. The city was coming to life.

Bannion was tired and gloomy, but something inside him had melted, something which had been frozen since Kate had died, and he now felt suddenly free and reanimated. He had found some small strength and sympathy left in him to give to Debby, and that meant he must count himself with the living instead of the dead.

The milk wagon in the next block was moving, and the clopping ring of the horses' hooves was a pleasant and familiar sound in the stillness. *"—My house being now at rest."* The lines of St. John came to Bannion unconsciously, and they seemed as fresh as the day he had first read them, and as strangely sustaining and familiar as the clattering horse in the next block.

Bannion turned onto Broad Street, and took a long, deep breath, enjoying the cold, misty air of the city. It was only his imagination, he knew, but it seemed to smell a bit cleaner this morning. Suddenly he remembered, he still had a present to buy for Brigid.

He stood for a moment or two, savoring the early-day sights and sounds of the city, and then he lit a cigarette and waved to a cruising cab. Something had ended this morning, he knew. Now he was starting over, not with hatred but only sadness.

That wasn't too bad, he thought.

The new detective series by L.V. Sims
featuring

SGT. DIXIE T. STRUTHERS

She's a cop. And she's a woman. Tough, yet compassionate, putting her life — and her heart — on the line...

__**MURDER IS ONLY SKIN DEEP**
0-441-81300-3/$3.50
The Department wants her fired. A lover wants her passion. A killer wants her dead.

__**DEATH IS A FAMILY AFFAIR**
0-441-14161-7/$3.50
A gruesome ritual murder plunges Dixie into a deadly web of occult terror.

(On sale December 1987)